A Table Before Me

Other Books by Debbie Viguié

The Psalm 23 Mysteries

The Lord is My Shepherd
I Shall Not Want
Lie Down in Green Pastures
Beside Still Waters
Restoreth My Soul
In the Paths of Righteousness
For His Name's Sake
Walk Through the Valley
The Shadow of Death
I Will Fear No Evil
Thou Art With Me
Thy Rod and Thy Staff
Comfort Me

The Kiss Trilogy

Kiss of Night
Kiss of Death
Kiss of Revenge

Sweet Seasons

The Summer of Cotton Candy
The Fall of Candy Corn
The Winter of Candy Canes
The Spring of Candy Apples

Tex Ravencroft

The Tears of Poseidon
The Brotherhood of Lies

A Table Before Me

Psalm 23 Mysteries

By Debbie Viguié

Published by Big Pink Bow

A Table Before Me

ISBN-13: 978-0990697176

Published by Big Pink Bow

www.bigpinkbow.com

Dedicated to several of my readers who deeply encouraged and motivated me while I was writing the last two books:

Alicia Paige Boggs, Amanda Morten, Amy Cooper, Baxter Waldron, Chrissy Current, Deanna Norris, Diane Woodall, Hollye Staley, Jan Geihsler, Julie Davenport, Karen Overstreet, Kathy Cole, Kirsten Fleming, Laura Kahapea, Patricia Ruments, Sabrina Wright, Sandra Lee, Stefanie Goodgame, Stephanie Chou, Stephanie Clapp, and Valerie Thompson.

1

Detective Mark Walters hated Mondays. It seemed like he always bled on Mondays. He picked up the birth certificate for Paul's son, wiped away the blood as best he could, then shoved it into his coat pocket. He turned to the unconscious banker on the floor. He had no idea why the man had attacked him, but he was sure that security was going to be on them both in a minute.

His phone rang. It was Liam.

"This is not a good time," he said without preamble as he answered the call.

"Sorry. Just thought you'd like to know the body of that secretary showed up, the one Cindy got her boss to confess to killing. Rose Meyer. Keenan just called and wanted to make sure you knew. Apparently he tried calling you first, but didn't leave a voicemail."

"Yeah, I've been a bit busy. Thanks, we'll talk more later."

Mark hung up.

Liam was finally out of the hospital and home recovering from injuries sustained when his girlfriend's stalker had attacked him. He was supposed to be out a couple more weeks while everything healed up. Mark had taken the opportunity to come to Sacramento and find the safety deposit box that his dead partner, Paul, had left a key to, and an encoded message about, with his ex-wife.

The man might be dead, but he was still finding ways to complicate Mark's life. The unconscious banker had jumped him after he'd brought him down here to the box, stabbing him in the shoulder in the process.

Mark kept waiting to hear running footsteps and shouting as security came charging in. This bank wasn't a branch of any chain he was familiar with, but when it came to security all banks pretty much functioned similarly. He listened, but there was only silence.

The wound was shallow, but there was too much blood for him to dream he could exit the bank without being seen. And that didn't even begin to take into account what would happen if someone found the banker unconscious while he was trying to leave. That and the security cameras that had a nice, clear view of his face convinced him that there was no way out of this except for through it.

The banker had a decorative kerchief in his breast pocket. Mark yanked it out and pressed it against his wound to slow the bleeding.

"Hey," he said, shaking the man with his free hand.

Mark had hit him in the head with his gun hard enough to knock him out. Hopefully he could get him awake and talking quickly. The man groaned and opened his eyes. Mark held his badge in front of them.

"Okay, buddy, so you just attacked a cop," he said, going on the offensive. "So, unless you're excited about some serious prison time, you're going to give me some answers."

"I can't," the man said, his features twisting.

"Sure you can. Let me help you out. This safety deposit box belonged to my partner who is now dead. You said that a woman was supposed to be coming for it. I'm guessing that would be his ex-wife. Well, she didn't want any part of whatever this is and so she dumped the key and everything else on me."

"You're Mark?" the man asked.

"Yeah. So, you've heard of me then?"

The man nodded.

"Then mind explaining the welcome stabbing?"

"He said it was possible you would be accompanying the woman. He didn't allow for the possibility that you'd be by yourself."

"So, this is the way you welcome all unexpected guests?" Mark asked.

"Only some," the man said with a groan as he eased himself up to a sitting position.

Mark stared at him. "What in the heck kind of bank are you running here? And why hasn't security come down here yet?"

"No one will be coming down here looking for us. In fact, no one will be coming down here at all until you and I leave the vault."

"I don't buy it. A guard is going to be checking these security cameras and when they see what's going on they'll come running."

"Again, no. I turned the security cameras off when we came down here."

"Oh, so they wouldn't catch you trying to kill me?"

"Yes, but believe me, it won't raise suspicion. It's a service we provide to select clients. Total privacy guaranteed."

"And Paul was one of those clients?"

"The box's former owner was, yes. I can't speak to his name. We assign top level clients codenames, for everyone's protection."

"Just how many criminals do you cater to?" Mark asked sarcastically.

"I really couldn't say because I don't know. Some, I have no doubt. Others have different reasons for valuing their privacy."

"How long has my friend been a client?"

"A very long time."

"Okay, what else can you tell me?"

"Only that if the wrong person came for his box we were to do whatever necessary to stop them from getting its contents."

Mark stared at the man. "You're willing to kill, go to jail, to protect your clients?"

"It's not an ideal scenario, but we do have a reputation to uphold. And the former owner of the box did reveal one or two details to one of the owners of the bank that were sufficient to convince them of the gravity of the situation."

Mark had never heard about something like this, at least, not in the United States. The fact that the bank was operating so brazenly in the state's capital shocked him. With the next breath, though, he realized that a number of the bank's high-level clients probably were high-ranking members of government.

He was not here to take down the bank, or even the guy who had attacked him. He had what he'd come for and now he just wanted to get out of there without involving the police.

"Since I have the key, and he mentioned my name, I guess I'm now the owner of the box," Mark said.

"Quite."

"What all does that get me?"

"What is it you're looking for?" the man countered.

"A way out of here without anyone noticing the fact that I'm covered in blood for starters."

The man smiled at him. "That can be arranged."

Mark shook his head. He felt like he'd somehow stepped into a whole other world that he knew nothing about. It baffled him, but, more than that, it scared him.

"So, arrange it."

~

It was Monday mid-morning and Cindy Preston was happy to be back at her old desk at the church. Things had been insanely busy, but at least things here were familiar. She knew what was expected of her. That was comforting, despite the chaos. There was something else, though, that seemed to be gnawing at the corners of her mind. She had a feeling as if she was waiting for the other shoe to drop.

Dave Wyman, the youth pastor, walked in the back door. She glanced up at him with a smile.

"How does it feel to be back?" he asked.

"Great, until I saw how messed up the Master Calendar is," she said, shaking her head.

"Yeah, good luck with that. I'm lucky; no one ever wants to use my room," he said with a grin.

"That makes you the only one who doesn't have a complaint about this," she said, hefting the massive binder in her hand.

"Hey, at least there's one person you don't have to try and make happy. I was happy just walking in here and seeing you."

"Thanks."

"Now we can get some more quiet around here."

She snorted. "I don't think things have been "quiet" ever."

"Well, certainly not for you, not for a few years at this point," he said. "You'll have to tell me if anything mysterious or exciting happened while you were away. You know, dead bodies, that sort of thing."

Cindy rolled her eyes.

"Aha, I have a feeling there's a story there."

"Speaking of mysteries, doesn't it seem like there should be a holiday coming up?" Cindy asked.

"Why?"

"I just feel a bit unsettled…and it's a bit frightening how often the mysteries coincide with holidays. So, I'm feeling, I don't know, something in the air."

"Well, there are a few holidays to choose between," Dave said.

"Like what?" she asked, frowning.

"Well, Arbor Day for one. It was last Friday, just a couple of days ago."

"Um, no," Cindy said.

She heard the office door open, but kept her eyes on Dave.

"There's Cinco de Mayo in a couple of days, oh and Ramadan starts in a few weeks."

"Neither of which I celebrate," Cindy said.

"How about tomorrow celebrating Yom Ha'atzmaut? Israel's Independence Day?" Jeremiah asked.

She turned, surprised that he was there. "How is that celebrated here?"

He shrugged. "Lots of ways. Pizza parties are popular. So are benefit concerts, barbeques, singing, dancing, flag waving, camel rides, you know, the usual," he said with a grin.

"I was unaware. It's not exactly what I had in mind, though," Cindy said.

"She's feeling like there should be a holiday coming up," Dave said.

"Ah, I see. Well, how about Lag BaOmer Day. It's the Sunday after next," Jeremiah said.

"Okay, you just made that one up," Cindy accused.

Jeremiah shook his head. "No. It's the thirty-third day of the counting of the Omer, which was a sheaf of barley or wheat. During the fifty days between Passover and Shavuot the people were to make an offering every day."

"So, why is the thirty-third day special?" Cindy asked, still thinking it sounded made-up.

"There are several theories about that dealing with miracles, or cessation of plagues, or pagan festivals. Whatever the origin, a lot of people take the day to celebrate. Young boys prepare to start learning the Torah, many get their first haircuts on that day. Couples get married," he said, a hint of suggestion in his voice.

"Oh no, you did a good job of reminding me the other day that I wanted the big church wedding so no quick ceremonies," Cindy said.

"Can't blame a guy for trying," Jeremiah said, giving Dave a wink.

"So, it's not lunchtime. What are you doing here?" Cindy asked. "I mean, I'm happy to see you."

Jeremiah smiled at her. "I'm glad to hear that. Actually, though, I'm here to talk a few things over with Wildman."

Cindy blinked and then looked from him to Dave. "Seriously?"

"Yup. Guy stuff."

"We could tell you, but then we'd have to kill you," Dave joked.

Cindy bit her lip to keep from saying something she shouldn't. Dave didn't know about Jeremiah's past. She had to remind herself not to say anything snarky in front of him.

Jeremiah managed to seem unfazed by the joke.

"Well, we can talk in my office," Dave said, turning to Jeremiah.

"Sounds good." He looked at Cindy. "And afterward we can go to lunch."

She grinned. "Sounds like a plan."

The two men turned and headed to the door. Dave held it for Jeremiah and just before exiting he turned. "Oh, you know what else is the Sunday after next? Mother's Day."

Cindy felt something cold and hard suddenly settle in the pit of her stomach. "That's the one," she whispered as he shut the door.

~

Jeremiah followed Dave to his office which was at the back of the youth room. As soon as they were both inside Dave shut the door and closed the blinds. It seemed overly cautious, but Jeremiah didn't say anything.

Dave waved Jeremiah to a seat on the couch and then went around his desk. He started to sit in his chair, then seemed to become agitated. He stood immediately back up. He rolled his chair around to the other side of the desk. He started to sit in it again then jumped back up.

Dave had gained the nickname Wildman because, like many youth pastors, he could be crazy and hyper with the kids when need be. His erratic behavior now, though, seemed a bit odd, even for him.

"Is there a problem?" Jeremiah asked.

Dave had asked to meet with him a couple of weeks earlier and this was the first chance they'd had to sit down. Jeremiah had no idea what the other man wanted to discuss, but his distress was clear.

"Yeah, switch seats with me. I mean, please," Dave said.

"Sure, whatever makes you feel more comfortable," Jeremiah said, standing up and moving so he could sit down in the chair.

Dave collapsed onto the couch with a heavy sigh. He looked like a man with the weight of the world on his shoulders. Worse than that, he looked defeated.

Jeremiah was still sometimes uncomfortable with the counseling aspect of his job. Some topics, some people, made it a lot more difficult than others. His heart went out to the youth pastor now, though. He was clearly in pain.

Jeremiah knew a thing or two about that.

"Thanks for agreeing to meet me here instead of over in your office. That would have raised too many flags, questions I'm not ready to answer," Dave said.

Jeremiah couldn't help but wonder if Dave was trying to avoid discussing whatever this was with the pastor. The man had already expressed a deep disapproval of Cindy and Jeremiah's relationship so it was easy to cast him in the role of prying villain for this purpose. It might be a bit unfair, but if Dave's issues had anything to do with the man then Jeremiah could relate.

"It's fine," Jeremiah said, offering what he hoped was a reassuring smile. "Now, what did you want to talk about?"

Dave passed a hand across his face. Whatever it was, it was tearing him apart.

"I haven't talked to anybody about this," he said, a tremor in his voice.

Jeremiah leaned forward and gripped his shoulder. Dave was lost on a sea of despair and confusion. He needed to talk, but was clearly afraid to. Why, Jeremiah wasn't sure. All he could do was try to ease that fear.

"I'm here to listen as a rabbi or a friend or as a fly on the wall who won't remember this conversation five minutes from now. Whatever you need. And whatever you tell me stays between us. And if you regret telling me afterward then I will lock it away where I keep the most private secrets in my mind and we will never have to discuss it again. Okay?"

"Okay, thank you," Dave said.

The man was sweating, but he visibly relaxed, slumping back into the couch. Jeremiah of all people knew that keeping a secret could feel like it was killing you, and telling a secret actually *could* kill you.

"My...wife...she...she wants a divorce," Dave said.

Jeremiah sat silent, waiting for Dave to continue. This wasn't what he'd expected, but it did explain a lot. The man had seemed distant, anxious since around Christmas. He'd been alone at the Valentine's dinner the church had thrown.

"She moved out a few months ago. I thought she just needed some space, time to think, but…it's over. That's what she says."

"What do you say?" Jeremiah asked softly.

"I don't know, that's the problem," Dave said, voice cracking. "She hasn't been happy in a long time. I've done everything I could think of to make things better. I offered to go to counseling, she refused. I've been attentive, spent time with her, tried to listen to her needs."

"And in all that listening, what did you learn?" Jeremiah prodded.

"That I'm not what she wants," Dave said. "She grew up in a small town where the preacher and his wife were admired, pillars of the community. The wife was invited to all the parties, the society events."

"The queen bee?" Jeremiah asked.

"Yes. I think when Sharna agreed to marry me she thought that someday that would be her, us. I told her when we were dating that I had no aspirations of being a head pastor. I like working with kids. It's what I want to do. I don't want to lead a church, deal with all the crap that a head pastor does."

There was quite a lot of crap dealing with kids that many head pastors couldn't deal with. Jeremiah didn't say that at the moment, though. It was better that Dave do most of the talking at this point.

"I don't know. I guess she thought I'd grow out of it."

"Only you didn't."

"No. And she's not getting to fulfill the role in the community that she wanted to. I've tried to make opportunities for her to be a role model for the kids, but she's just not interested."

"So, you've learned that she doesn't want you."

"Yes."

"Do you still want her?" Jeremiah asked.

"I did. I've fought so hard to keep her. I've done everything she's asked. I even started talking to the Presbytery about the possibility of becoming an associate pastor somewhere in the area, moving on from being a youth pastor."

"Have you done all of this because you love her, the woman she is, or because she is your wife?" Jeremiah asked.

Dave hesitated. "Does it matter?"

"At this moment in time, a great deal."

"I used to love her, with everything that was in me. I couldn't imagine a day going by without her."

"And now?"

"Now, I've had days, sometimes weeks without her. And I'm starting to question, to wonder if I was as mistaken in her as she was in me. Was this always the person she was and I was too blinded by emotion to see it? Or has she changed?"

"It is rare that people actually change. What is far more common is that with time they become more of who they already were, both the good and the bad."

"Unfortunately, I'm having a hard time seeing the good I used to love in her."

Jeremiah cleared his throat. "I've never been married, so there are some things I can't speak to from experience. If you can't see the good, though, and you've been trying, then maybe it's not there anymore or maybe she can't access it given her current situation."

"Her current situation?"

"Some people aren't good for each other. For a marriage to work, it has been my observation that both people have to work, to sacrifice, have to care more about the other person than they do about themselves."

Dave nodded glumly. "You're right. I've seen it time and time again. I've given similar advice to my kids. Sometimes they go off to college and they come back a couple of years later on break or whatever, and they come and talk to me about the guy or girl they found. I tell them what you just told me."

"Dave, be honest with yourself for a moment. What do you want?"

"I want things to be the way they were seven years ago."

"And do you see any way that can happen?"

"No."

"So, if you can't have that, what do you want?"

"I want this nightmare to be over. I'm tired of fighting to keep her when she so clearly wants to go. I thought at first she was running to see if I'd chase her. I chased and she just got more angry, more hateful. She doesn't want to stay and I don't see any way that either of us can be happy at this point if she does."

"So, why are you fighting letting her go?"

"Because she's my wife. It's like you said. It's not because I love her, not who she is now. It's because I made a commitment to her before God and I feel the need to honor that. Besides, how can I be an example for the kids if I'm divorced?"

The anguish was there in his voice at the end. Dave already knew he had lost her. Part of him was willing to accept that, but he couldn't accept the thought of what it might do to the youth who looked up at him.

"Dave, if I've noticed for months that something is wrong, then you bet the kids have noticed. You honor your commitment to being a role model for them by going through this with grace and dignity and being honorable in your actions and words. You will never say a bad word about her to them. You will always show respect toward her because she has been your wife. Your actions will speak volumes. Those who know you, have spent time with you, will understand that this is not your fault. And if you can emerge from this, better, stronger, more committed to your calling, then I think you and they will be just fine."

Tears began to stream down Dave's face. He had known the answer. He needed someone else to agree with him before he could face the reality of it all.

"I won't fight her on the divorce," he said.

"I don't think you should. I think you've done all the fighting you could to keep her. Anything now will just harm you and those around you."

"You're right," he said.

Dave wiped away the tears and suddenly he was sitting up straighter. A look of peace came over him and he actually looked better than he had in months. He stood abruptly. "I've got to call her and let her know. Then I'll tell the staff this afternoon. They deserve to hear it from me before the gossips hear and start spreading it around."

"Okay," Jeremiah said, standing as well. "If you need anything, I'm here."

"Thank you, rabbi. I appreciate you taking the time to see me. You've been more help than you could know."

"You're welcome."

"Do me a favor?"

"What?" Jeremiah asked.

Dave locked eyes with him. "I've come to see more clearly my own situation over the past months and one thing has stood out to me in stark contrast. I don't think Sharna and I were necessarily right for each other. We weren't seeing each other for who we truly were. We were each enchanted with who we thought the other person could be. What really helped me see that is watching you and Cindy together. I've never seen two people more right for each other. When you proposed to her, I was honored to be one of the witnesses and I knew at that moment that what I felt for Sharna was just a pale shadow of what you felt for Cindy and she felt for you. Hold her tight. Never let her go."

"I won't," Jeremiah said, suddenly feeling choked up himself.

"Good, because I'll hold you to that. Now, go take your fiancée to lunch while I call my wife and tell her I'm done."

Jeremiah felt the pain of that moment fiercely for just a second as he imagined their roles reversed. It took his breath away and he knew then that despite everything, despite who he was and what he'd done, he could never let Cindy go. Not even to save her.

2

The banker had been true to his word. He'd managed to get Mark some bandages, a new shirt and jacket which were both far nicer than the ones that were ruined, and sent him on his way in about ten minutes. It was remarkable, actually. After leaving the bank he had debated his next move.

He had the name of the woman who had been the mother of Paul's child. He wanted to get to work tracking down mother and son as quickly as possible. He finally decided that the best thing he could do was get himself to a medical clinic and get the wound taken care of.

The doctor there looked at him askance when he said that he'd suffered an unfortunate incident with a steak knife. Mark had finally flashed his badge at him and the man seemed more cooperative and less likely to report him to the local police.

Once he was stitched up he hit the road, heading for home. He'd slept for a couple of hours the evening before and gotten up just after midnight so that he could be at the bank by the time it opened in the morning. Now as he headed for home he closely monitored his condition. Aside from a painful throbbing in his shoulder, which probably was helping to keep him awake, he seemed to be doing okay.

In the time they'd worked together, Paul had never once really talked about the Dryer family money. Nor had he ever really acted like he came from money. Technically, he didn't. When he'd assumed the real Paul Dryer's life, though, the money had come with it.

Clearly it was that money that had granted him access to a place like Five Diamond Bank. He couldn't help but wonder just how far the bank went to protect its clients' assets. Given the knife he took to the shoulder he was guessing there was more than one skeleton in the organization's closets. Literally.

When he was younger he probably would have felt duty bound to do something about that. Now, though, he found himself appreciating that there were places that understood that some secrets were best kept.

He had at least gotten something out of the place. Paul had gone to great lengths to hide the existence of his son who had been born when Paul was twenty-four. That meant the boy would be about thirteen now. Paul had certainly never given any indication that he had a son. He was pretty sure the news would come as a shock to his ex-wife as well.

The mother's name was Sadie Colbert. He had been wracking his brain trying to figure out where he knew that name from. Suddenly, in the middle of nowhere on the 5, it came to him.

Sandra Colbert was one of the children that had been kidnapped by the cult. Her body had never been found. The news reports he'd read had mentioned that Sandra had a twin sister named Sadie. His stomach lurched as he made the connection. Paul had a child with the sister of one of the kidnapped kids. Since he was the cult leader's son he had almost certainly had some contact with Sandra. He maybe even knew how she had died. Mark felt like he was going to be sick. What on earth could have possessed Paul to look up the girl's twin and then start an affair with her? He didn't know where Sadie Colbert was now, but he knew he had to find her.

~

Cindy had a nice lunch with Jeremiah despite the fact that he'd been less talkative than usual. She didn't ask what he and Dave had discussed. Privately she hoped that, whatever it was, Jeremiah had been able to help him. She'd been starting to grow concerned about Dave. He'd seemed off...depressed or something for a while.

When she made it back to the church she had quickly discovered why as Dave gathered together the entire staff to announce that he and Sharna were getting a divorce. Cindy felt bad for him. She didn't know what had gone wrong, but she did know that Sharna had been showing up to church events less and less over the last eighteen months or so. She couldn't even really remember the last time she'd seen her.

Cindy had cried and hugged Dave. The rest had expressed their condolences, even the pastor whose face was otherwise unreadable. She just hoped he didn't make problems for the youth pastor. He already had enough to deal with without Ben coming down on him.

The rest of the work day everyone had been quiet. It was not exactly a great first day back to work, but, in truth, there was no such thing as a "normal" work day at the church. Then again, the feeling of dread that had been quietly gnawing away at her insides since Dave mentioned

Mother's Day grew more intense as soon as she stopped trying to fix the Master Calendar for the day.

She was home and she'd just finished eating dinner when her phone rang. She really was on edge. She tried to tell herself that she was being unreasonable, paranoid.

It was her father.

The knife twisted more in her gut as she answered.

"Hey, Dad."

"Hey, Sweetie."

"What's up?" she asked. "Everyone okay?"

Usually it was her mother who called, and most of the time it was to tell her something about her brother, Kyle, and his latest exploits. She found herself suddenly breathing a prayer that they were both alright.

"Yup, everyone's fine. You know, I've got some time off and we were thinking this might be a good time to take a little trip."

"Oh, where are you going?"

"Pine Springs."

"Oh! Here? You want to come here?" she asked, startled.

"Yeah. We've never really been out to see your place. And we've never gotten to really spend any time with Jeremiah."

"Oh, I see," she said, mouth going dry as she could feel herself starting to panic a little.

"Figured with Mother's Day coming up we could kill two birds with one stone, so to speak."

"Oh, well, that's great," she said.

"Glad you think so. Kyle liked the plan. He's going to come spend time with all of us."

"Kyle is coming. I see," she said.

Things had gotten a lot better between her brother and her, but that didn't mean they were perfect. She hadn't seen him since he'd been in the hospital and broke up with his own fiancée. He'd made no bones about his dislike for Jeremiah either and that's when she and Jeremiah had just been friends.

She could feel panic begin to set in.

"Cin? You okay?"

"Yeah, sorry, I was just thinking. When will you all be arriving?"

"Well, we're set to fly in Saturday if that works for you. We're going to stay about ten days."

"Great. I mean, I'll be having to work. Since I just got back to the church I can't really take time off."

"That's fine. We're adults, I'm sure we can find ways to amuse ourselves during the day," he said drily.

"Of course you can. And we can all visit The Zone one of the weekend days. It will be fun," she said, hoping the strain wasn't showing in her voice.

"Wonderful. I have to go, your mother needs me for something. I'll see you in a few days."

"Love you, Dad."

"Love you, too."

She hung up the phone and forced herself to take several deep breaths. She needed to call Jeremiah and Geanie. They'd understand. They both knew her relationships with her mother and brother were complicated.

She called Jeremiah first and he answered right away.

"I miss you," he said.

"I miss you, too," she said, struggling to keep the tension out of her voice.

"What's wrong?" he asked.

She took a deep breath. "I just got off the phone with my father. He, my mother, and Kyle are coming to spend time here and to celebrate Mother's Day. They want to get to know you."

"It makes sense. Now that we're engaged they want to know what you've gotten yourself into."

"I'm glad you sound so calm, I'm freaking out."

"Trust me, so am I. Frankly, I'd rather kill Kyle than spend even an hour with him and my brief introduction to your parents wasn't exactly under the best of circumstances."

"It's going to be okay, right?"

"Yes."

"Thanks," she said.

"And if not, you can throw darts at Kyle's face. For real," he said with a touch of dark humor.

"I haven't had his picture on my dartboard for a while."

"I know."

"How do you know? That dartboard is on the back of my bedroom door."

"I've been in your bedroom since you took it down."

"When?"

He chuckled. "Would it make you feel good or bad if I said I've been in there several times, watching you sleep?"

"Both, actually."

"Okay. I checked your house for any kind of surveillance equipment after we got back from Israel."

"Was there any?"

"No."

"That's a relief."

Her phone beeped in her ear.

"I've got another call coming in."

"Go ahead and take it," he said.

"Okay."

She answered the incoming call which was from Liam.

"Hi, Liam, how are you feeling?"

"Better, how are you?"

"Okay."

"Has Mark had a chance to call you yet?"

"No, why?"

"They found the body of a young woman. They think it's Rose Meyer."

Cindy's throat tightened. "Oh."

"Do you know if there's someone we could have go down to identify the body? As I understand it her only living relative passed away a few months ago."

"Yes, her grandmother died," Cindy said, throat constricting more as she realized she was fighting back tears. How sad was it that she was the expert the police were having to call when she hadn't even known the other woman? "I thought she had a roommate, the one who reported her missing."

"She did. That young woman was killed in a car accident a few days ago. Another victim of the 405."

"Oh, how terrible," Cindy said.

She'd been on that freeway half a dozen times, enough to know that if she could avoid it she did so at all costs. Fortunately, she didn't have to be down in Los Angeles and Orange Counties very often. It was the nice thing about Pine Springs. They were in Southern California, but they had a bit of distance between them and all the crazy.

"Yes, and it's left us scrambling to find someone who can give a positive identification for Rose."

"There was a friend, at work, who cared for her. He could probably identify the body."

"What's his name?"

"Beau. I'm sorry, I don't know his last name or have his contact information, but he works at Rayburn NextGen Solutions. He shouldn't be too hard to track down."

"That's great. Thanks."

"You're welcome."

Tears stung her eyes. Beau had been in love with Rose. She hated the thought of him having to be the one to identify her body. He was probably the best qualified to do so, though. The tragedy of it was hitting her hard. Rose had been so alone. That was why Cartwright had been able to prey on her.

"Everything okay?" she asked Liam, trying to take her mind off of it.

"I'm fine. Sorry that Mark didn't call you earlier about this. He's been hard to reach today."

"Is he alright?"

"I think so. He was following up on something having to do with Paul," Liam said, voice guarded.

"Oh, I understand," Cindy said.

"Anyway, it sounds like a good time to be recuperating. I guess they found two separate bodies today. The first one was early this morning."

"In the same place?" Cindy asked quickly.

"Doesn't sound like it. You have a good night."

"You, too."

She was just about to call Jeremiah back when the house phone rang, startling her. She got up and crossed to the kitchen where it was hanging on the wall.

She picked it up.

"Hello?"

"Will you accept a collect call from-" a mechanical woman's voice began.

"Leo Rayne," a man's voice burst in, sounding frantic.

Her mind froze for a moment. The name was familiar. Who was it? Leo. Leo. *The guy from the next cube at my last temp job*, she realized.

"Yes, yes," Cindy said hastily, mind racing.

A couple moments later she heard a click.

"Hello?"

"Cindy! Thank heavens. You have to help me. They've arrested me for murder!"

3

"What?" Cindy blurted out.

"It's true! They just grabbed me as I was leaving work. I'm at the police station. They said I killed this girl. I don't even know her. You have to help me."

"Leo, why are you calling me? You should be calling a lawyer," she said, totally bewildered and more than a little freaked out.

"I don't know any lawyers. The only person I know that can help me is you," he said, sounding desperate.

"Me? How on earth can I help you?"

"You solve mysteries, catch killers. Like Mr. Cartwright. You have to help me," he begged.

"Leo, calm down, I'll see what I can do to help. You need a lawyer, though."

"A lawyer can't find the real killer! Please, help me, come down here and just let me tell you what's going on. She's some stripper. I don't go to strip clubs. I don't know what's going on."

"You're at the police station?"

"Yes."

"Okay, I'll be down there in a few minutes. Just, try to keep it together until then."

"Okay, thank you. Hurry. Please."

"I will."

She hung up and called Mark, but his phone went straight to voicemail. She left a message and then called

Jeremiah who agreed to pick her up and go with her to the police station. Then, after a moment's hesitation, she called Liam back.

"Cindy, what's up?" he asked, clearly surprised.

"I just got a really weird call from a guy at my last temp job. He said he's been arrested for murder and he begged me to come down to the police station and help find the real killer."

"That's bizarre. Did you call Mark?"

"It just went to voicemail."

"Well, unfortunately I can't meet you down there, but I'll keep trying to get hold of Mark and see exactly where he's at. I expected him to be back in the area by now."

"Thanks. Jeremiah is going to take me down there."

"Good. I think all of the detectives down there at least know who you are."

"I'm sure we'll manage," she tried to reassure him.

"Okay. Call me if things get too weird."

"I will," she said before hanging up. She had to shake her head, though, wondering exactly what would be "too weird" in his estimation. After all, the situation was already too weird in hers.

Jeremiah arrived in just a few minutes and they were soon on their way to the police station.

"Who is this guy?" he asked.

"He sat next to me at that last job. I'm baffled that he called me."

"Do you think he did it?"

"Honestly, I don't know. I've met a lot of killers that I wouldn't have thought were."

"Some are good at hiding it," he said.

She turned quickly, hoping he hadn't taken what she'd said badly. He was scowling slightly.

"I'm not talking about you," she said, putting a hand on his arm.

"No, you knew I was a killer straight off," he said.

"You're not a…you're a good guy, not some vicious murderer. And the only reason I knew anything was because I saw you shoot that monster before he could kill me."

He glanced at her. "No, you knew before that. In the church when you screamed and I came running. You saw me and freaked out. You tried to get away from me."

"I thought the killer heard me screaming."

"A killer did hear you screaming. Just not the one you thought."

There was something wrong. Normally he didn't fixate on the subject to this extent. "Are you okay?" she asked.

"I'm fine…actually, I'm not. I've been thinking about your family's visit. Your dad's a smart guy. And your brother already dislikes me. And your mom was so fixated on your brother last time that I actually have no idea what to expect from her, but I'm prepared for it not to be pleasant."

Cindy took a deep breath. "I know it's going to be a stressful few days, but honestly, what's the worst that can happen?"

"We end up in the middle of some murder investigation, with life and death consequences, and your whole family gets a glimpse of the real me, freaks out and forbids you to marry me."

"That's not going to happen," Cindy said.

"Really? How do you know?"

"I mean, what are the odds? I'm sure there won't be any craziness or mysteries or anything while they're here, just a lot of uncomfortable dinners."

"Really, no mysteries, huh?"

"Yes."

"And we're going to the police station right now because you're not going to help out your former coworker and solve the mystery of who really killed this girl?"

Cindy flushed. "I'm sure it's all just some misunderstanding. Or he is guilty. At any rate, we've got until Saturday before my folks show up."

"I'm not feeling better."

She turned to look at him. "It doesn't matter what does or does not happen while they're here. There's nothing they could ever do or say to keep me from marrying you."

He was quiet for a moment, his jaw clenched, his eyes straight ahead on the road. Finally he whispered, "Promise?"

"I promise."

She could feel him relax slightly.

"It could just make all future encounters awkward," he said.

She laughed. "Nothing can prevent that and it has nothing to do with you," she said.

He smiled at that.

"Better?" she asked.

"Better," he agreed.

Which was a good thing since they were pulling into the parking lot at the police station. He parked and they got out of the car. She took his hand.

"You know I love you, right?" she asked.

"God only knows why," he said.

She kissed him.

"Because He made you for me."

He shook his head, but he was smiling now. "Sometimes I think you're crazy," he said, his voice teasing.

"Crazy in love," she affirmed with a wink.

Hand-in-hand they walked into the police station. It was funny. She'd been there before, knew or had met a lot of the people who worked there, and yet she still found the place to be intimidating and uncomfortable.

They walked up to the reception desk. "We're here to see Leo Rayne," she told the officer on duty. The officer nodded, picked up a phone and spoke into it. Moments later he hung up. "Have a seat and someone will be with you shortly," he instructed them.

They went and sat in a couple of chairs. Jeremiah slowly rubbed his thumb across the back of her hand. He looked calm, relaxed, serene even. She could feel the tension in his fingers, though. He didn't like being there any more than she did. Truthfully he probably liked it a lot less since he'd done things that most of the people here would lock him up for in a heartbeat. They were lucky that the police officer who knew the truth had never tried something like that.

A minute later a man wearing a suit walked over carrying a file folder. He extended his hand. "Hi, I don't think we've ever officially met. I'm Detective Keenan. You must be Cindy and Jeremiah."

"How did you know?" Cindy asked as she stood and shook his hand.

"You two are pretty famous around here. Plus, I know that Leo was ranting about calling you, that you'd fix everything," he said. "You must be pretty close."

"Actually, no. We worked together for three days."

Keenan's eyes widened. "Wow. And you were his one phone call? You must have made one heck of an impression."

"I don't know," she said, glancing at Jeremiah who just nodded slightly.

"Follow me," Keenan said.

They wound their way through the police station. A few people waved at them as they went by and Cindy waved back, struggling to remember names. Oftentimes she saw these officers at crime scenes but had never really been introduced to them. She did know that all of them had dropped what they were doing at one point, though, to help track her down when she'd been kidnapped by bad guys pretending to be F.B.I. agents.

They arrived at an interrogation room. Inside, sitting at the table, was Leo. His wrists were handcuffed together. His clothes were in disarray and he looked awful. He turned and when he saw her he jumped to his feet.

"Cindy, please you have to help me."

"Sit down!" Keenan barked.

Reluctantly Leo did as ordered.

Cindy went and sat across the table from him. She felt a bit of trepidation in doing so, but reasoned that there really wasn't anything he could do to her with Jeremiah so close by.

Jeremiah leaned against the wall, watching everything like a hawk. She focused her attention on Leo.

"Tell me what happened," she said.

"I was getting ready to leave work this afternoon when all of a sudden these policemen showed up. They told me I was under arrest for the murder of some woman."

"Her name is April Snow. She was an exotic dancer."

"I don't know her! I've never even heard the name!" Leo burst out.

"Then why do they think you killed her?" Cindy asked.

"I don't know, something about my fingerprints. I keep telling them I had nothing to do with this, but they won't listen."

Leo was so agitated he probably wasn't comprehending even half of what the police were saying to him. She couldn't blame him. She turned and looked at Keenan for more information.

"His prints were found all over the crime scene, including on the victim."

"They showed me a picture of a dead woman," Leo interrupted.

"Do you have a picture of her from when she was alive?" Jeremiah asked.

The detective nodded and pulled a picture out of the file he was carrying. He handed it to Jeremiah who looked at it for a moment before stepping forward to hand it to Cindy.

The young woman in the picture was smiling. She had curly auburn hair, hazel eyes, and pale skin. Cindy put the picture on the table and slid it toward Leo.

"Are you sure you've never met her before?" she asked, "even in passing somewhere?"

"I don't know anyone named April Snow and I don't know any strippers," he said.

"Just look, please, and think if you might have seen her at the grocery store or a restaurant, anything," Cindy said.

31

"We need to figure that out before we can set about clearing you," she said.

She didn't know yet if Leo was innocent but his distress seemed real enough.

"Okay," he said, seeming to calm slightly at her words.

He looked down at the picture and stared at it. "I don't know her," he repeated.

"I know, but have you ever seen her? Even once? It's important. Remember, she might have had different hair, been wearing sunglasses, so really look at everything."

"Her teeth look familiar," he said after several seconds had passed.

"Her teeth?" Cindy asked, glancing at Jeremiah. That seemed like a really random thing to notice.

"Yeah, the incisors, they're really pointed, like little fangs, like an animal or vampire or something."

"And that's familiar?" she pressed.

He nodded. "I don't remember faces easily unless there's something that stands out. I think I've seen her teeth before and thought that they looked like fangs."

It was something at least. "Do you remember where you were when you noticed her teeth?" she asked.

He squinted at the picture, staring for about a minute. Finally he lifted his head. "No, it's really fuzzy, more like I dreamed about seeing her teeth instead of actually seeing them."

She glanced up at Keenan. "The picture of her dead that you showed him, were her teeth visible?" Given his current state of mind he could be remembering her teeth from that other picture and that would certainly make things seem fuzzy.

Keenan opened the folder and looked at something. "No, they were not," he said.

"Okay, so now we just have to figure out where you've seen her," Cindy said, turning back to Leo.

"I don't know," he said, voice breaking slightly. "I'd tell you if I did."

"That's okay, we'll figure this out," she said soothingly. She looked again at the detective. "Could we have a couple of minutes?" she asked.

His presence wasn't doing anything to help calm Leo down.

He nodded. "I'll go get us all some coffee. I'll be back in a few minutes," he said.

"Thank you."

As soon as he left she turned back to Leo. "Leo, why did you call me?" she asked.

He looked up at her. "The next day at work, after Mr. Cartwright was arrested, everyone was talking about it, how you'd figured out that he killed Rose. I was shocked. It had never occurred to me that she was dead. One guy was talking about how you always solve mysteries. That night I looked you up online. I saw some of the articles about you, like the one with the serial killer that you stopped. I'd seen those headlines before. I just never realized that was you. I was bummed I had missed my chance to watch you solve a crime. Then, today when they arrested me I kept thinking how crazy it was. No one was listening. I knew it was a mistake. I thought of you. I figured if you could find a killer when no one even knew a murder had happened then you could for sure find out who really killed that girl."

"Okay. I'm going to do my best," she said, forcing a smile.

"Thank you."

"Have they told you anything else? When she was killed? How she was killed?"

"If they did I can't remember. Then again, the last couple hours have been a blur," he admitted.

"I know, it's okay. I'll find out."

"Thank you for coming, for believing in me," he said.

"You're welcome."

Before they could say anything else the detective returned with the promised coffee. Cindy would much rather have had a soda, but she was willing to take the caffeine however she could get it at the moment. Jeremiah's words about her family's visit were echoing in her head and she felt a burning need to make sure that this was all wrapped up before they got there.

She was also increasingly certain that Leo was going to be no help. At least, not at the moment. "Leo, I have to go, but I'll see you tomorrow. I'm assuming they're holding you here overnight," she said.

She glanced at the detective who nodded.

She stood and then reached across the table and squeezed his hand. "I know it will be hard, but try to get some sleep tonight."

There was panic in his eyes. He didn't want her to go, but there wasn't anything more she could do for him in that room. She had a lot more questions but they were for the detective and she didn't need to be asking them in front of Leo at the moment.

"Okay," he said.

They left the room, the detective closing the door after them.

"I have some questions," Cindy said to him.

"Okay, let's go sit at my desk," he said.

They followed him to his desk and as soon as they were all seated Cindy asked, "When was the victim killed?"

"The medical examiner is working to figure that out. The body was found early this morning. We haven't even been able to figure out yet when was the last time someone saw her. We think she lived in Los Angeles, but we haven't been able to confirm that yet."

"You told Leo you found his fingerprints, where?"

The detective cleared his throat, looking like he was about to clam up.

"You need to tell him because if you have, he doesn't remember. And, once he knows I'll know," Cindy said.

The detective sighed. "We found his prints on her purse, on her wallet, and on her throat. She was choked to death and his were the hands that did it."

4

Jeremiah had to admit it didn't look good for Cindy's former coworker. Men had been convicted on far less.

"How do you know she was a stripper?" Cindy asked.

"Excuse me?" Keenan asked.

"You don't yet know where she lived or when she was last seen. How do you know that she worked as a stripper?"

"She had business cards in her purse. Plus the medical examiner recognized her. Apparently she worked his cousin's bachelor party a few weeks ago."

"Bachelor party!" Cindy blurted out, eyes growing wide.

"Yeah, a bachelor party," the detective repeated.

"No, there was a bachelor party that Leo went to two weeks ago. It was odd because it was on a Tuesday night. It was for a coworker who is now behind bars. He killed his secretary, Rose. Her body was found today, too."

Detective Keenan leaned forward. "Now that is a very big coincidence," he said. "Did Leo say what happened at this bachelor party?"

Cindy shook her head. "He couldn't remember most of the night. He was pretty hung over the next day."

"So, he might not remember killing the girl."

Cindy flushed. "I don't think he did kill her. If you want a suspect, look at Cartwright. It was his party and he'd already killed another girl just a couple of days before."

"So what motive would Cartwright have to kill the stripper?"

"What motive would Leo have?" Cindy countered.

"I don't know, but his prints are on the body and Cartwright's aren't."

"Cartwright was getting ready to marry an heiress. He killed Rose to cover up the fact that he'd had a relationship with her and she was pregnant. Maybe something happened with the stripper and then he panicked and killed her to keep that quiet, too," Cindy said.

"And this happened without any of his buddies seeing it? Because otherwise they'd be liabilities, too, by that logic," Keenan said.

While that seemed a bit thin, Jeremiah would agree that if a known killer had come into contact with the stripper that the police should be taking a hard look at him. Still, he understood what Keenan was saying about the physical evidence pointing elsewhere.

"How was Rose killed?" Cindy burst out.

A muscle in Keenan's jaw twitched. "I don't know. That's not my case," he said.

"But you can call the medical examiner and find out. I mean, if they were killed in similar ways then Cartwright starts to look more and more suspicious," Cindy pushed.

"Okay. Visiting hours are over," Keenan said, standing abruptly.

"Excuse me?" Cindy asked, clearly taken aback.

"I was willing to hear you out, see if you could get the suspect to incriminate himself, as a professional courtesy to Liam and Mark, but I am officially done."

"I don't understand," Cindy said.

"He wants us to go," Jeremiah said.

She gave him a quick glare. "I understood that part. What I don't understand is why. Is he afraid that we'll make him work too hard?"

Jeremiah stood and practically picked Cindy up out of the chair. "She's tired. It's been a long day," he said to the police officer who was starting to turn slightly red in the face. "Thank you for your time."

"But, we're not-"

"Yes, we are," Jeremiah said, interrupting her protest.

He hurried her to the parking lot as fast as he could. Once inside the car she turned on him. "Why did you do that?"

"Because he was getting really angry. And if we want to continue to live in this town, and occasionally stop bad guys, we need to not piss off the local police."

"That guy was a complete idiot," Cindy fumed as Jeremiah started the car and pulled out of the parking space.

"No, he was just doing his job. The evidence is very one-sided."

She scowled at him, eyes flashing with anger. "Don't you dare take his side over mine!"

"I'm not taking his side. I'm just pointing out that he was not unreasonable to draw the conclusions he did."

"And I am?"

Just like that Jeremiah realized he was standing in the middle of a mine field. He had underestimated just how upset Cindy was, and clearly she was ready for war on the topic.

"No, I could see your point very clearly," he said carefully.

"So, whose side are you on?"

"Your side, always," he said, holding his breath.

"And don't you forget it," she said.

"Never." He took a deep breath. "I think we're both used to dealing with Mark who knows us and can think outside the box."

"Mark will be able to tell me how Cartwright killed Rose," she said.

"Yes. And tomorrow we can talk to him all about it."

~

Mark woke up just in time to swerve out of the way of the oncoming headlights. Cars roared past him, honking as he eased back onto his side of the road. Adrenalin raced through him. He was in worse shape than he thought he was. Even worse, he was still two hours away from home.

With his heart pounding like a jackhammer he debated what he should do. He already had music blaring and the air conditioning going full blast. He called Traci.

"Hey, hon, are you almost home?" she asked, her voice hopeful.

"I'm still two hours out."

"Is everything okay?" she asked.

She was always quick to pick up on how he was feeling.

"Not really. I'm falling asleep at the wheel."

"Okay, then you need to pull off the road and find a motel room for the night," she said, voice full of concern.

"I'll be okay. Just, talk to me for a little while," he said.

"I don't want you to wind up dead because you were too stubborn to stop."

"I said talk to me, not lecture me."

"Fine, how did the trip go?" she asked.

"I found the safety deposit box."

"What was inside?"

"A birth certificate. Paul had a son."

"That was the big secret?" she asked after a pause. She didn't sound nearly as shocked as he had been.

"Yes. Think about it. Given how much he was hiding, he would have wanted it kept a secret from both his father, the crazed cult leader, and the Dryers."

"Well, where is the kid?"

"I don't know. All that was in there was a birth certificate. I got the mother's name off it, though. It's Sadie Colbert. She's the twin sister of one of the girls the cult abducted."

"Now that's just creepy," Traci said.

"I thought so, too."

Talking was good. It was helping him wake up and clear his head. He thought about telling her about the crazy banker, but since he'd actually been stabbed it was best that he wait until he got home and she could see for herself that he was alright.

"How are the babies?" he asked instead.

~

Cindy was still fuming about Detective Keenan so Jeremiah decided to change the topic.

"Where are your parents staying?" he asked.

"With me. I'm going to have to get an inflatable mattress or something for the guest room."

He glanced at her. "You mean my office?" he asked, trying not be territorial and failing.

"Yes, sorry."

"No, that makes sense. Unless you were going to have them stay at Geanie and Joseph's, which could get awkward," he said.

He had half hoped she'd take the idea and run with it. Instead she said, "Kyle can sleep on the couch in the living room. It makes out into a bed."

"Okay," he said.

He shouldn't be feeling as agitated as he was. He was intensely private for a reason. Given that he'd just painted the spare room and claimed it as his future office, it felt like an invasion that other people were going to be staying there.

No, it wasn't that others got to stay there. It was that he didn't get to.

He sighed in frustration. He kept wishing that they hadn't opted for a long engagement and that they could get married right away.

Preferably before everyone gets here.

He had to admit he was worried that they were going to disapprove of him and his relationship with Cindy. Given how things had gone with his own family he knew why his anxiety was so high. He believed Cindy when she said that nothing they could say would change her mind. He had to hold onto that, no matter how stressful things might get.

"I figure we can all go to The Zone either Sunday, the day after they get in, or Saturday, the day before Mother's Day."

"Sounds good. Kyle should love some of the daredevil stuff in the Extreme Zone," Jeremiah said. "Unless it turns out to be too tame for him."

"I used to love roller coasters when I was little, before…" she trailed off.

Jeremiah knew she was thinking about the death of her sister, an event that had haunted and shaped the rest of her life. Despite that, he still didn't know what exactly had happened to Lisa. One day he would push her to tell him, but not today.

They arrived at her house.

"Do you want to come in for a few minutes?" she asked absently.

"Sure," he said.

He didn't want to leave before he felt like she was calmer. He understood her agitation, but he didn't want her to still be angry at him and not able to deal with it until later.

He followed her inside and as soon as the door was closed he pulled her into his arms and kissed her. "Are we okay?" he asked afterwards, keeping hold of her.

She looked up at him. "Yes," she said, a small smile teasing the corners of her mouth upward.

"Good. Anything else I should know about?"

"Ummm, nothing that I can think of."

"Okay, then. Shall we continue to plan for the invasion?" he asked as he let go of her.

She sighed. "Probably. We should go out for brunch on Mother's Day. Where do you think would be nice to go?"

"I think we should go somewhere that you love," he said.

"Yeah, but it's Mother's Day so I want to pick somewhere my mom will like."

"Well, you're a mother to Blackie, so pick somewhere you'd like, too," he said with a grin.

She smiled. "Does this mean you want to go out to brunch on Father's Day because you're a father to Captain?"

"Nah, Captain and I are more like brothers-in-arms," he said.

"Ah, yes, I can tell the resemblance. Two warriors just hanging out being buddies," she teased.

"Don't forget swapping war stories. That part's very important."

"I'm sure," she said, rolling her eyes.

She turned and headed into the living room, and after a moment he followed her. She sat down on the couch with a weary sigh and leaned her head back. "I don't have time to just sit still," she said.

"Why not?" he asked as he sat beside her.

"I've got too much to do. I've got to find a killer and get the house ready for company."

"I can help."

"With which one?"

"Both."

She tilted her head forward and looked at him. "You'd help me clean the house?"

"Why not? They're not going to be seeing my place, so no cleaning required there. Besides, they're going to be my relatives soon enough."

"I like the sound of that," she admitted. "You're hired."

"Thursday is my day off. I can spend all day here if you want."

"That sounds heavenly. That means I don't have to get started tonight," she said.

"Which is good. You can get some rest instead."

"I could use it."

"And it's probably time for me to hit the road so you can get it," he said.

"Okay," she said.

He stood up and headed for the door. Cindy followed him after a moment. He gave her a quick kiss before heading out.

Once outside his hand lingered on the door of his car and he paused before opening it. The hair on the back of his neck was standing on end. He turned around quickly, scanning the surrounding area for something or someone. There was nothing but darkness.

And silence.

It was too quiet. He stood for a moment more, debating what to do. Slowly things began to feel like they were returning to normal. A dog barked a few houses down, he heard a neighbor's television set blaring some sitcom, and a car rolled noisily down the street, clearly in need of some sort of engine repair.

He forced himself to let go of the breath he'd been holding.

I'm just jumpy because I know in a few days Cindy's family will be here, he told himself. A lot of extra prayer was going to be in order to try and keep himself calm and collected during their visit. He loved Cindy for so many reasons. He loved that she had reached past his defenses and opened the floodgates of emotion that included love and joy and passion. Unfortunately, once opened those gates did little to repress the other emotions that he needed to.

He forced himself to get into the car. He drove home which fortunately wasn't too far. Although he kept checking his mirrors he couldn't see anything unusual. He had just parked in his driveway when his phone rang. He pulled it out of his pocket and frowned when he saw that it was his secretary, Marie, calling.

Marie rarely called him after work hours. "Marie, is everything okay?" he asked, tensing as he answered the call.

"Rabbi! Have you heard?" she asked, a note of hysteria in her voice. "About the synagogue?"

"No, what about the synagogue?" Jeremiah asked.

"It's on fire."

5

"What?" Jeremiah asked, praying he'd heard Marie wrong.

"The synagogue is on fire!" Marie half-sobbed.

"When?"

"Now."

"I'll be right there," he said, heart pounding.

"Wait, let me get you the address," she said.

"The address? Marie, is it our synagogue that's on fire?" he asked, confused.

"No, the one across town. On Highland Ave. The one I grew up in."

Jeremiah felt relief surge through him. It was still terrible news, but he was grateful it wasn't their synagogue. It was easy to see, though, why Marie was so distraught.

"I've driven by it. I'll go over there and see if there's anything I can do to help," he said.

"Thank you," she sobbed. "I have to call my cousin."

"Okay. I'll talk to you soon."

It took Jeremiah twenty minutes to get to the other synagogue. Three firetrucks and a news van were already there. The building was still on fire but it looked like the crews were getting it under control. He parked down the block where he'd be out of the way and then walked up on foot.

One of the firefighters was talking with an older couple. Jeremiah was fairly certain the gentleman was the synagogue's rabbi. From their body language he would guess that the woman was his wife. He walked up and stood a couple feet away, waiting to be recognized. Finally the man turned to him. "Yes?"

"I'm sorry for the intrusion. I'm Rabbi Silverman from across town. I came to see if there was anything I could do to help."

"Rabbi, I have heard of you. I'm Rabbi Yaakov," the other man said, extending his hand.

"Jeremiah," he said, shaking it. "My secretary, Marie, grew up in this synagogue. Her maiden name was Bernstein."

"Ah, of course. I remember her. It was a shame about her brother a few weeks ago."

"Yes, it was," Jeremiah said.

It had not been an easy few weeks for Marie, that was certain. He was afraid that the burning of her old synagogue would just make everything that much worse.

"What happened here?" Jeremiah asked, indicating the burning building.

"I wish I knew," Yaakov said, his voice sorrowful. "Hopefully the firefighters can tell us what happened."

It was morbid, standing there and watching the building burn with them, but he stayed. Sometimes just having someone else around at a time like this could bring comfort, a sense that one wasn't alone. At least, that was what he had observed. He had felt alone almost his entire adult life. Except when he was with Cindy.

He finally pulled out his phone and called her.

"Hey, what's up?" she asked, sounding like he'd woken her.

"Sorry, honey, did I wake you?" he asked.

"No, it's fine, I'm okay," she said, yawning in the middle of it.

"I just wanted to ask if you could put it on your prayer list that the Jewish synagogue on Highland has caught fire. They've almost got it contained, but there's still a lot of damage. I'm here to offer my help and support as well as that of our…my synagogue," he said.

"That's terrible!" she said, seeming to come fully awake. "Of course, I'll tell everyone. And please let them know that we're here to help if they need anything."

"Thank you, I'll let them know," he said. "Goodnight."

"Goodnight," she said.

He hung up and turned back to the rabbi and his wife.

"You were talking with your wife?" Yaakov asked.

"No, my fiancée," Jeremiah said.

"Ah, congratulations."

"Thank you. She said if there's anything their church can do to help, to please let them know."

The other man tilted his head to the side. "She does not work at the synagogue where you are the rabbi?"

"No, she's a secretary at the church next door. First Shepherd on the corner of Main and Lincoln."

"You're marrying a Christian?" he asked, his voice laced with surprise.

"I am," Jeremiah said, steeling himself.

"You're a brave man," Yaakov said after staring at him for several seconds.

"Thank you. And we are both serious. If there is anything either of us can do to help, we are more than happy to do so."

"We appreciate it. A lot will depend on how much damage has been done," Yaakov said, turning again to look at the building.

There was no longer any evidence of flames, but smoke was still pouring out of the structure.

"At least there's still a building in front of me," Yaakov said. "When the synagogue my cousin goes to in Los Angeles caught on fire last year there was nothing left."

"That's terrible," Jeremiah muttered.

"You're from Israel?"

"Originally."

"Then you've seen many things more terrible," Yaakov said.

Jeremiah remained silent. It was true. He had. Daily he struggled to forget.

~

Mark heaved a sigh of relief as he pulled into his driveway. It was good to be home. He sat in the car for a minute, calming himself. Traci was going to be plenty upset when she found out he'd been stabbed.

He checked his phone. There were three messages from Cindy and at least half a dozen messages from Liam that he hadn't even listened to yet. He was tempted to ignore them until the morning, but his partner didn't usually bother leaving more than one message. Something important had to be going on.

He called Liam.

"Mark, are you okay?" Liam asked as he answered the phone.

Mark winced as his shoulder started throbbing harder. "Mostly. Aren't you supposed to be on bed rest still?"

"I am, or, rather, I would be if you hadn't been so hard to get hold of today."

"What's going on?"

"They found Rose Meyer's body."

"Ah," Mark said. "Was someone able to positively identify the body?"

"Yes, thanks to Cindy. She knew which one of Rose's former coworkers to tap for that."

"Great. So, it worked itself out."

"Ummmm…."

"What, did something else happen that I missed?" Mark asked wearily.

"Another body was found earlier today. It had fingerprints on the throat. It turns out they belonged to another employee at that place Cindy was temping."

"Another one?"

"Yeah, a guy by the name of Leo. Apparently after officers took him into custody he used his one phone call to call Cindy."

"What, why?"

"That's exactly what Detective Keenan was wondering."

"Keenan? How did he get involved?" Mark asked.

"He was assigned to the case when the first body showed up this morning."

"Did it show up in the same place as the other body?"

"No, it did not."

"What are the odds that two different people at Cindy's temp job were murderers and killed women and hid their bodies within a short period of each other?"

"Pretty staggering. That's why Cindy likes Cartwright for the murder of the other woman as well."

"She told you that?"

"Yeah, she called me after she got back from the police station when she couldn't get hold of you."

"Sounds like I picked a heck of a day to go out of town," Mark said with a sigh.

"Pretty much. Did you at least find something?"

"Yeah, I did," Mark said, hesitating to elaborate. "I'll explain more later," he finally said. "I made it home. I'll deal with all of this in the morning."

"Just please call both Cindy and Keenan tomorrow."

"Will do. Get some rest."

Mark hung up and headed into the house. As he closed the door behind him Traci came flying in from the other room. She was about to throw her arms around him when she abruptly stopped short.

"That's not your jacket or your shirt," she said.

"That's true," he said.

"So, what happened to yours?" she asked.

"They got ruined, a minor… puncture."

"You got shot!"

"No, of course not," he said, trying to speak soothingly. "Oh."

"I got stabbed."

"What?"

"It was no big deal. More of a misunderstanding, really," he said.

She pounced on him and began to unbutton his shirt. "Show me right now," she growled.

"Here, let me do it. It's a nice shirt and I don't want the buttons ripped off," he said.

"Fine," she snapped, stepping back and folding her arms across her chest.

Mark shrugged out of the jacket and handed it to her. She took it without a word. Then he worked to finish unbuttoning his shirt. He tried not to grunt in pain as he took it off.

Traci's eyes narrowed anyway so he must have winced. She took the shirt and tossed it with the jacket on the arm of the living room sofa. Then she stepped forward and inspected his bandages.

"What happened?" she asked.

"Turns out that's a real exclusive bank where Paul had the safety deposit box. They don't take kindly to being surprised by someone showing up that they didn't expect."

"I told you to tell them you were a police officer."

"Honestly, I'm not sure that would have changed things much."

"Where did you get the new shirt and jacket?"

"From the same guy who stabbed me."

She raised an eyebrow. "Okay, that deserves explanation."

"I'll tell you the whole thing if I can get some pain killers and something to eat."

She folded her arms and continued to stare at him.

"Okay, I'm telling you everything regardless, but can I please get some pain killers and food?"

"Alright. Come into the kitchen," she said. "I can't wait to hear all about this crazy banker."

~

Cindy struggled with trying to go back to sleep after Jeremiah called. She finally gave in and got up. She thought about getting on the computer and seeing if she could do any kind of research about the woman Leo had supposedly killed.

She was awake, but she wasn't thinking that clearly. Given that the woman had been a stripper, Cindy decided that maybe going onto the web and trying to look up info on her might be a bad idea. Some things once seen couldn't be unseen and she had no desire to come across unsavory pictures.

She got herself a glass of orange juice, and then wandered into the room that was going to be Jeremiah's office. She needed to get a couple things to make it a serviceable guest room for when her parents arrived.

She walked over to the closet and opened it, wanting to see if there was stuff she should move out of the way. Her eyes fell on a box in the corner and she felt her stomach clench. There were a few odds-and-ends in that box, things that she hadn't found any place or use for and yet couldn't bring herself to part with. In it was her sister's jewelry box.

She knew from a conversation she'd had with Kyle a while back just how deeply their mother still missed Lisa. In the days after her sister's death, their mom had made Cindy go through her sister's stuff and get rid of almost all of it.

The only things that she knew for sure had survived were the T-shirt Lisa had been wearing the morning of the day she died and the jewelry box and its contents. Kyle had the T-shirt. Cindy had never known that until she was with him on the cattle drive vacation that had turned out so nightmarishly for everyone.

Maybe enough time has passed that Mom would like something of Lisa's, the thought came to her. It had been roughly two decades, maybe it was time they both dealt with her sister's death.

With shaking hands Cindy opened the box. She moved stuff around in it until she could reach the jewelry box which was at the very bottom. She pulled it out and held it in her hands, staring at it for a long time. Finally she stood and carried it into the living room and set it on the coffee table.

She wanted to open it. Desperately.

But she didn't want to do it alone. She went and got her phone from her nightstand. It was a little after ten. She'd gone to bed earlier than usual because she had been so tired from the day. Now, though, she felt like she would never be able to sleep again until she had done this.

Geanie was always up late. She didn't know about Joseph, though. She texted her friend.

R U Up?

Geanie called back within seconds. "What's up, are you okay?"

"Yeah, I'm fine, it's just…it's a bit hard to explain. Look, I know it's late, but could you come over for a little while?"

"Of course! I'll be right over."

Cindy didn't know how many traffic laws Geanie violated, but the other woman showed up in record time. She walked in wearing a pair of Mickey Mouse pajamas.

"See, I knew I was dressing appropriately for the party," she said, indicating Cindy's pajamas.

"Yup," Cindy said, giving her friend a quick hug.

"Now, what's up?" Geanie asked as she followed her into the living room.

"This is," Cindy said, pointing to the jewelry box as she sat down on the sofa.

Geanie sat next to her and studied the box. "Okay, you've got me. Is it boobytrapped or something?"

Cindy laughed. "In a way, yes."

"Okay, that was your laugh that you laugh when you might cry instead," Geanie said.

"You're right. This jewelry box and the stuff in it belonged to my sister. It's all I have of hers, and, besides an old T-shirt, all any of us have."

"Wow."

"And I haven't been able to open it since the day I took it from her room and hid it in mine so it didn't get thrown away."

"That's intense. So, why think about it opening it now?"

"I guess I thought it was just time to stop being afraid of a jewelry box. I was also thinking that maybe my mom would like something from it for Mother's Day. At any rate, I felt it was time, but I didn't want to do it alone."

Geanie hugged her again. "I'm right here for you. What are you planning on doing with the jewelry? Wearing it?"

"I don't know. Maybe. Maybe I'll donate some of it or give it away. I mean, jewelry is made to be worn, not locked away in a box somewhere."

"When my great-grandmother died when I was little, there were boxes and boxes of her costume jewelry to go through. My mom and I ended up turning it into a game as we went through, picking out pieces we wanted, bartering for other pieces. It felt good and more like a celebration. It was like we were pirates divvying up the loot. Maybe you and your mom could do that."

"No, I don't think either of us would be up to doing that, particularly not together. It does sound like fun, though," she said, feeling a bit wistful.

Geanie shrugged. "It was just a suggestion. Now, let's get this baby open."

Cindy nodded, took a deep breath, and reached out to open the box. Inside she stared at a riot of color. Over the years everything had jostled and become completely jumbled together. She reached in and pulled out a ring with a plastic pink plumeria on it. A tiny rhinestone sat in the center of the flower. She held it up, a flood of memories coming back to her unexpectedly.

"Mom and Dad brought this back for her when they went on a trip to Hawaii. Funny, I can't remember what they brought Kyle or I, but I remember this ring. It was so Lisa. She wore it a lot."

"As she should have. It's beautiful," Geanie said.

On impulse Cindy turned and slid it on Geanie's right ring finger. It fit perfectly.

"You should have it," Cindy said. "It's very you as well."

"I couldn't take your sister's ring," Geanie protested.

"No, please."

Cindy exhaled deeply. Somehow it felt as though a tiny weight had been lifted. She was starting to realize that she had not been treating these things as treasured memories, but rather as stones around her neck that she was afraid would drag her down beneath the water.

With Lisa.

She shook her head. "You were right, just not about who I should be doing this with."

Geanie tilted her head questioningly.

Cindy took a deep breath. "No more sacred cows."

She grabbed the box and dumped everything out onto the coffee table. "Let's divvy up the booty."

Geanie laughed and clapped her hands excitedly. "Aye, aye, captain."

They spent the next hour laughing and trading as Cindy told her the stories she could remember about some of the pieces of jewelry. Remembering didn't hurt like she was worried it would. Instead it felt good. Lisa was in heaven. One day she'd see her again. Until then she needed to start celebrating the time they'd had together instead of mourning the time they didn't.

"Oh, this one," Cindy said, holding up a gold heart locket. "Mom gave it to Lisa for her tenth birthday. She put a picture of the two of them in it. That night Lisa put in a picture of the guy in her class that she liked. Mom saw it a couple of days later and was so disgusted. She thought Lisa was too young to be 'chasing boys'. For the next year they kept changing the picture in it. It was like the end of Sleeping Beauty where the fairies keep arguing whether her dress should be blue or pink."

"That's hilarious! What is it now?"

Cindy smirked. "I know the answer." She opened it to reveal a picture of Kyle as a little boy.

Geanie laughed out loud. "Is that your brother?"

"Yup. Mom said if she wanted to look at a boy she could look at him. She glued the picture in."

"Oh, that's priceless!"

"Yup. I'm going to give this to Mom. It should make her think of both Lisa and Kyle."

"And with Kyle's picture in it, how could she not love it?" Geanie asked.

"I know, right?"

"That's a perfect choice." Geanie bent over what was left of the unsorted pile. "Oh, and I think I see something else that would be perfect."

"For my mom?"

"No, for you."

Geanie lifted up a blue heart necklace.

"The Titanic necklace. Lisa loved that movie. It was one of her favorites. I always thought it was depressing."

"Me, too. Don't get me started," Geanie said. "I have all sorts of problems with it. However, everyone loves the necklace."

"Yeah. I might have hated the movie, but I always was a bit envious that Lisa had the necklace."

"And now you have it."

Cindy shook her head. "I don't have anything I can wear this with. It's so big and eye-catching."

"I know exactly what you're going to wear it with," Geanie said, voice cracking slightly.

Cindy turned to her sharply. Geanie was smiling, but tears were shimmering in her eyes.

"What should I wear it with?" she asked.

"Your wedding dress," Geanie said softly. "It can be your something blue."

Cindy threw her arms around Geanie and suddenly they were both crying. "It's perfect," she sobbed against the other woman's shoulder.

"I know," Geanie said. "I saw it and I just knew. I could see you wearing it on your wedding day."

"Thank you for everything," Cindy said. "I couldn't have done this without you."

"You're welcome. I think your sister would be thrilled to know you're going to wear it when you walk down the aisle."

Cindy pulled back and wiped her eyes. "And this is why you're my Matron of Honor."

"Don't you forget it," Geanie said, dashing away her own tears.

6

Jeremiah was up early the next morning. He took Captain and headed to the park to get some exercise for both of them. It felt good to stretch his legs and run. The big German Shepherd clearly agreed because he gave an occasional happy bark mid-stride as he kept pace with Jeremiah.

For his part Jeremiah tried not to think about the synagogue that had burned the night before, or Cindy's family coming into town, or whether or not Leo was a murderer. As he ran he tried to let the world fall away.

After several laps of the park Jeremiah slowed to a walk. Captain walked happily next to him, tongue lolling. They stopped at the water fountain which had a newly added fountain at dog height. Jeremiah smiled as he watched Captain lapping at the water.

Thirst slaked they continued walking, making their way slowly back toward the car. They had almost made it there when Jeremiah noticed a figure sitting very still on a park bench nearby. The man was wearing a trench coat and gloves. Jeremiah tensed.

As he approached the man turned his head just enough so that Jeremiah could get a look at his face. It was Martin, the C.I.A. agent.

Jeremiah went and sat down on the bench beside him.

"Beautiful dog," Martin said.

"I'm going to have to find a different park," Jeremiah said. "Unpleasant things always seem to be happening in this one."

"Yeah, but if unpleasant things can't find you here, they might track you down somewhere else, like your office," Martin said. "It's better this way."

"What do you want?" Jeremiah asked.

"I was in the neighborhood and thought I'd check in on my favorite cousin," Martin said.

"You didn't have to go out of your way."

"It wasn't out of my way. *At all.*"

Jeremiah tensed more. "Something I should know?"

"A couple local bullies are working hard to acquire themselves a very big stick."

"How big?"

Martin glanced at him sideways. "Massive."

Jeremiah's blood ran cold. "And the odds of them getting that stick?"

"Better than I'd like."

Jeremiah took a deep breath. "Why tell me?"

"You know what they say, if you see bullying happen, you should speak up."

"And what makes you think I'll be able to return the favor? I don't run into many bullies these days," Jeremiah said.

"One of them might decide to run into you. His brother was a wedding crasher you knew."

"Does he know where to find me?"

"As far as I can tell, no."

Jeremiah took a deep breath. "So, how about you tell me where to find him?"

"I would love to, truly. Unfortunately, there are complications."

Jeremiah clenched his fists. "So, you expect me to do nothing?"

"I expect you to be careful. I also expect you to pick up the phone if I call."

"If I find him…" Jeremiah said, letting the threat go unspoken.

"I know. There won't be anything anyone can do to help the outcome."

"As long as we're clear."

"Crystal," Martin said.

Martin stood to go.

"One more thing," Jeremiah said softly. "You weren't anywhere near Cindy's house last night, were you?"

Martin frowned. "No, why?"

Jeremiah shook his head. "Probably nothing."

"Well, if it turns into something, you know my number. Take care of yourself. You really are my favorite cousin, you know."

"Thank you," Jeremiah said.

Martin nodded and took off across the park at a brisk walk.

Jeremiah sat for a moment, pondering what Martin had just told him. The C.I.A. had uncovered a terrorist plot to get a weapon of mass destruction into southern California. They couldn't close in on the terrorists just yet, though, without fear of losing the weapon in the process. So, it was a waiting game. One that was especially dangerous for Jeremiah since at least one of the terrorists already had it in for him.

He sighed heavily as he got up. Days like this he regretted the fact that he was retired.

~

Mark was heading into the precinct early the next morning. He decided to call Cindy and get her version of the events the night before first. Fortunately, she answered her phone.

"I hear I missed some excitement last night," he said after exchanging greetings.

"Detective Keenan doesn't know what he's talking about," she burst out. "There is no way that Leo killed that…woman."

"I haven't had a chance to speak with Detective Keenan yet. I wanted to hear your side first. Liam just gave me the barest of details."

"The body of a woman turned up yesterday morning. They found fingerprints on her throat that belonged to Leo. He claims that he doesn't know her."

"And you believe him?" Mark asked.

"I do. After he saw a picture of her alive, though, she did seem vaguely familiar to him. There's a lot that still has to be figured out, like when exactly she was killed," Cindy said.

"And what will that tell us?" he asked.

"We're acting under the belief that she was the stripper at Cartwright's bachelor party two weeks ago. Leo was at the party but most of the evening is a blur to him. If we find out she was at the party and that she was killed that night, then I think we need to be looking at Cartwright for a second murder."

"Two murderers at one party that don't have a connection to each other is a stretch," Mark said.

"That's exactly what I said!"

"How do you account for Leo's fingerprints being on her neck?" he asked.

"I don't know yet, but I'm sure we'll figure it out. We need to talk to Cartwright and whoever else was at that party. Leo could tell you the name of the best man. He threw the party and would have been the one to hire the stripper I would think."

"Stands to reason."

He could hear her breathe a sigh of relief on the other end of the phone. Clearly she had really hated dealing with Keenan. He didn't blame her.

"Thank you," she said.

"Keenan is lead on that case, we're still going to have to include him," Mark said.

"Unless we can prove quickly that it's tied to the other case," she said.

"Wow, you really didn't like him, did you?"

"He had his mind made up already and refused to listen to reason."

"I'm sorry. I'll see if I can get him to play ball."

"I would appreciate it. I just don't think Leo could be the killer."

"Okay. Well, have a good day back at the church and I'll keep you posted."

Mark pulled into the precinct right as he was hanging up. As soon as he made it inside he tracked down Keenan who was at his desk handling paperwork.

Mark sat down in the chair next to the desk. "How's it going?"

"Okay. It would have been better if you were reachable yesterday," he said with a frown.

"Fishing trip. I was out of cell service all day," Mark said.

"Well, I'm glad you're back. I was dreading the thought of having to deal with those two again today."

"Which two?"

"Cindy and Jeremiah."

"Ah," Mark said. Clearly the ill feelings were mutual. "I understand the suspect used his one call to contact Cindy."

"Yup and she came down here all gung ho, determined to prove that he was innocent despite what the evidence said."

"Maybe he is."

Keenan rolled his eyes. "Don't start with me."

Mark shrugged. "Just trying to cover all my bases."

Keenan looked like he was about to say something rude. Mark quickly changed the subject before he could.

"Thanks for babysitting the Rose Meyer case. I hear her body turned up yesterday."

"Yeah. I tracked down one of her coworkers last night, a guy named Beau. He's going to help identify the body this morning."

"Great, thank you."

"You're welcome."

"Anything else I should know at the moment?"

"No. Just waiting for the full reports to come back on both bodies."

"Okay, keep me in the loop."

"Ditto, dude," Keenan said.

Mark stood up and made his way over to his own desk. He had a lot of work to do, but he also had one burning question he needed answered.

~

The synagogue that had caught on fire the night before was all anyone seemed to be talking about at the church. Every person who came in the door asked Cindy if she'd heard about it, and if their church was helping out in any way. She kept smiling and saying that she'd heard and that there was no word yet on what the synagogue needed.

"We should make a little sign so you can just point to it," Geanie said around eleven. "It would be faster."

"I know. It's nice that everyone is concerned and wants to help."

"It would be even nicer if we knew how to help."

"Exactly," Cindy said.

"I see you're wearing the purple bracelet from last night. Good for you," Geanie said, changing the subject. "It looks good."

"Thank you. It feels good," she admitted. "I noticed you were wearing the pink plumeria ring."

"Guilty as charged," Geanie said.

The door opened and Dave came in, looking a little beleaguered. Cindy was wondering if it had to do with his wife. "Everything okay?" she asked.

"No," he said, throwing himself down in the chair in front of her desk.

"I'm sorry. Is there anything we can do to help?"

"Not unless you can magically conjure me up four more counselors for the summer camps," he said.

Cindy winced. "Yeah, that's not going to be easy."

"Tell me about it," he snorted.

After the crisis a couple years before at Green Pastures, the camp that the church used, getting adults to agree to chaperone the camps had been incredibly difficult. It didn't matter that they weren't even using the same camp. No one wanted to be even tangentially involved.

"I mean nothing can possibly go more wrong than it has in the past, so what are they afraid of?" he asked.

"That things go even half that badly," she suggested.

"Which would still be really, really bad," Geanie chimed in.

"Thanks for that," Dave said with a scowl. He sighed overdramatically. "If only there were two brave, beautiful, mature women who I knew that could be counselors," he said.

He looked up at them.

"Sorry, I'm not brave," Cindy said.

"And I'm not mature," Geanie said.

Dave laughed. "Three years ago, maybe, but now? I mean, Cindy, you solve mysteries, get shot at and kidnapped by bad guys and don't even break a sweat. Geanie, you're married, a pillar of the community, and getting ready to have kids of your own."

"Where did you hear that?" Geanie demanded, turning red in the face.

Dave tilted his head and stared at her with a puzzled look on his face. "I thought...I guess I must have heard...I don't know," he floundered. He quickly turned back to Cindy. "Come on, Cindy, remember when you drove the kids delivering those Thanksgiving dinners a couple of years ago? That worked out well."

"No, Dave," she said in as stern a voice as she could muster.

"Come on," he pleaded. "Think of the kids."

"I am thinking of the kids. I'm thinking how much they'd hate having me for a counselor and vice versa," Cindy said.

"But-"

She held up her hand. "The only way I'd even consider it is if you first got Jeremiah to agree to go as a counselor. Just how likely do you think that is?" she asked with a smirk.

Dave looked so crestfallen that she couldn't help but feel sorry for him. Not sorry enough to change her mind, though.

"Geanie? It would be fun. You'd get to do all kinds of crazy things. You could even get your cabin to raid one of the others and I'm sure I'd look the other way."

Wow, he must really be desperate, Cindy thought.

"No," Geanie said, anger seething in that one little word.

"Fine," Dave said, dragging himself to his feet. "But mark my words, we're going to end up calling everyone in the directory if I don't find some people soon."

He left and as soon as the door shut Geanie said, "*He* can call everyone in the directory. I won't be helping with that. You shouldn't either."

"Are you okay?" Cindy asked.

"No, I'm not. I'm going to kill Joseph."

"Why?"

"Because that's the only person who could have told Dave that we were trying to have kids."

"So, you *are* trying to have kids," Cindy said softly.

Geanie nodded. "It's supposed to be a secret."

"Well, I won't tell anyone."

"Jeremiah knows. He's the only other person."

"How long has he known?" Cindy asked.

"A few weeks."

"Now there are two guys in trouble," she muttered.

"Don't be mad at him. We told him it was a secret," Geanie said.

"Maybe Dave just guessed. I mean, you and Joseph have been married a little over a year. It's natural that people start making baby assumptions," Cindy said.

"Maybe you're right. Maybe I'm jumping at shadows. Anyway, I should probably be more upset at the other thing he said."

"What?"

"He said I was mature," Geanie said, wrinkling her nose. "When did that happen? I never wanted to be the mature one."

"Yeah? I never thought anyone would call me the brave one," Cindy said, rolling her eyes.

"What's happened to us?"

"I guess we've changed."

"At least being brave is a good thing," Geanie said glumly.

"Not necessarily. The bolder I get the more risks I take. That's not always a good thing," Cindy said, thinking of some of the close calls she'd had in recent months.

"That's still better than being mature. I'm supposed to be the crazy, wacky one."

"Trust me, Geanie, you'll always be the crazy, wacky one."

"Promise?"

"I do."

"It just bothers me. Am I losing my flair, my spontaneity? I mean, how many weeks has it been since I've worn something truly outrageous to work?"

"Since it's been a few weeks since I've been here, I can't say," Cindy said.

"See, you shouldn't have to think about it. You should be able to say, 'Of course you wore something weird last week. You wear something weird every week.'"

Cindy bit her lip. "I think maybe you've just been distracted and had your mind on other things."

"That's no excuse. I'm going to wear something truly outrageous this week to make up for lost time. I'll show Dave."

Cindy tried to imagine what Geanie would consider truly outrageous and had to give up. Her imagination wouldn't stretch that far. She'd just have to wait and see.

"Yeah, you will. He'll rue the day he ever called you mature."

The office door suddenly was hurled open. A woman stepped inside, a snarl twisting her features. "Where is she?" she demanded in imperious tone.

"Where is who?" Cindy asked, taken aback.

"I'm looking for that no good home wrecker, Cindy Preston."

7

"I'm Cindy Preston. What on earth are you talking about?" Cindy asked.

"I'm Nita Rayburn," the woman said, striding forward.

"Cartwright's fiancée," Cindy said, as she slowly stood up.

"Former fiancée thanks to you and all your meddling. How could you?"

Nita's hand flashed and pain exploded across Cindy's temple as the woman slapped her hard.

Out of the corner of her eye she saw Geanie lunge to her feet with a cry.

"I saved you from marrying a murderer. You should be thanking me," Cindy burst out.

"Thanking you? For destroying my happiness? Are you insane?"

She pulled back her hand as though to strike again. Before she could, Geanie was there and she caught Nita's wrist in her hand.

"I think you better sit and calm down," Geanie said, her voice menacing.

"How dare you touch me?"

"How dare you strike this woman without provocation?"

"I told you, she ruined my happiness."

"You came here, seeking her out. Now get hold of yourself before I have to call the police," Geanie said.

"Do you know who I am?"

"Yes, but you don't know who I am and right now that should worry you."

Something about Geanie's tone clearly got through. Nita turned and really looked at her then abruptly sat. Geanie let go of her wrist and stepped back. "Now that's better," she said.

Nita blinked at her then turned back to Cindy. "I love Kenneth. We were going to get married."

"I'm sorry, but he cheated on you and then killed the girl when she got pregnant."

"That's not true. The police have her real killer in custody."

"It is true. He confessed. And he tried to kill me," Cindy said.

"You misunderstood the whole thing. He was trying to explain to you, to cover for his friend, Leo."

"Leo?" Cindy burst out.

"Yes. He worked with Kenneth. The police arrested him last night for the murder of another girl. He was the one who killed that secretary."

Cindy was torn between anger and pity. She tried to keep both out of her voice as she answered. "I'm sorry, but Leo didn't kill Rose. It was Kenneth. He confessed to it and he even shot another man the night the police captured him."

"No, you've got it all wrong. Leo killed both of them. The police will prove that and then Kenneth will be free. Of course, the wedding was ruined. Why? Why did you do it? What did we ever do to you?"

"You didn't do anything to me, but Kenneth killed a woman."

"You should be thanking her for exposing him before you married him. Otherwise you'd be the wife of a murderer, and not only would it be humiliating but it would also take a whole lot of money to fix that," Geanie intervened.

"You're wrong, both of you."

Cindy was still struggling to understand what was happening. "Why are you here?"

"To look you in the eyes and tell you that Kenneth didn't do it. You are a monstrous woman and soon everyone will know it."

Nita stood abruptly, turned, and stormed out of the office. The door slammed shut behind her.

"What just happened?" Cindy asked.

"A close encounter of the crazy kind," Geanie said.

~

Mark had been able to look up the file on the Sadie Colbert kidnapping. After the discovery of the bodies of some of the kidnapped children a couple years before, officers had reached out to the family to give them an update. There was a phone number and they resided at the same address as they had back when the girl was kidnapped.

When lunch rolled around he headed for his car. He tried the number, but it was disconnected. A lot of people were getting rid of their landlines, so he decided to go to the house next before searching for further information.

The house was in an upscale neighborhood, although it had fallen into some disrepair. It was probably once the showplace of the block and now it was the proverbial dog on the block. A real estate investor would probably love to get their hands on it and do something with it.

He went up to the door and rang the bell. He saw a curtain in the front window move and then the door was slowly opened by a woman with gray hair and haggard appearance.

"Mrs. Colbert?" he asked.

"That was my mother," she said.

He blinked in surprise. "Sadie Colbert?" Mark asked.

"Yes, why?" she replied, folding her arms over her chest.

She was painfully thin, almost gaunt. She looked ill, maybe it was the waxy pallor of her skin or the dark smudges under her eyes. She might once have been attractive, beautiful even, but time and care had ravaged her. He found himself trying to wrap his head around the fact that she and Traci were the same age. Sadie looked like she could have been Traci's ailing mother.

"I'm Detective Mark Walters. I wanted to talk to you about my former partner, Paul Dryer."

She flinched at the name and for a moment he thought she was going to slam the door in his face. "I don't want anything to do with him," she said in a hoarse whisper.

"Well, you won't have to have anything to do with him. He died about two years ago."

"Oh," she said, her eyes getting wide. "What happened?"

"He was killed in the line of duty."

She nodded. "So, he became a police officer?"

Clearly whatever had happened between them Paul must have broken off all contact shortly after the birth of the child. "Yes, he did. He was a detective."

"He would have been good at that," she said, her head bobbing up and down on her thin neck almost involuntarily.

"He was. I need to ask you some questions about him."

"I haven't seen him in thirteen years. I don't think there's anything I can help you with. Good day," she said, stepping back and starting to shut the door.

"I know the two of you had a son."

She froze and he could see the pulse in her throat begin to jump. "How did you know that? No one was supposed to know that."

She craned her neck and looked around, as though worried someone might have overheard. He took his cue from that.

"Perhaps it would be best if we spoke inside," he said.

She hesitated a moment and then nodded, clearly afraid that if she tried to turn him away he'd just continue talking out there where someone might hear what he had to say. Her fear was so palpable that he struggled with the sudden urge to look over his shoulder to see if anyone was watching.

He followed her into her house. She shut and bolted the door then led him back to a living room. There were lots of lamps everywhere, pushing back the darkness. Every window had heavy curtains drawn over it and looked like they were never opened. He was getting a clear image of Sadie as a woman who valued her privacy.

She sat down in a straight-backed chair that had seen better days. The furniture all looked to be what once must have been very high-end but now seemed shabby from age and misuse. He sat down on the sofa. On the coffee table was a picture of an older couple, her parents from the resemblance.

"Are your parents still alive?" he asked.

"No. Mother died many years ago. Father contracted cancer a couple of years ago and I moved back to take care of him. He died over the summer."

"I'm sorry for your loss," he said. "Where were you living before that?"

"Elsewhere," she said in clipped tones.

He smiled at her. "It will take me only a couple of minutes to find that out and it's of no great importance."

She took a deep breath. "Denver. I lived in Denver for a little over ten years."

"So, you moved there right after you had the baby?"

Her lips tightened, but she nodded.

"And where is the child now?" he asked.

She looked at him in surprise. "How should I know?"

Mark leaned forward. "You didn't raise him?"

"Of course not. I was twenty-one, an idiot school girl who made a stupid mistake. I wasn't about to jeopardize my whole future over that."

"So, you gave him to Paul?"

"I thought you said you knew Paul," she said, suddenly suspicious.

"I did, but not as well as I would have liked. He left me information after his death that it's taken me a while to decipher. I only just found out about the boy a couple of days ago."

"Paul was beside himself when I told him I was pregnant. He became agitated. He started ranting that his father couldn't find out about it. I gathered he was quite afraid of him. No, when the baby came, we left it at a police station. Sanctuary, that's what Paul called it."

"You gave the baby up?" Mark asked, heart sinking.

"Yes."

"Did you leave his name with him or anything that would identify him?"

"Of course not. Paul was terrified someone would find out it was his."

The baby went into the system without so much as a name. Now, thirteen years later it could well be impossible to find him. Mark was fairly certain the father Paul had been ranting about was his real one and not the one he had conned into taking him in.

He realized that he'd come to Sadie's home expecting to see a boy who looked like Paul living there. Even though he was thwarted in finding Paul's son there was still valuable information she could give him that would help fill in the gaps.

"Did you know who Paul was?" he asked, hoping that he'd be able to tell how much she actually knew.

"I knew his family was wealthy. So was mine…at the time."

"Did you know about his past, his childhood?" he asked.

She took a deep breath. "Are you asking if I knew he'd been abducted by the same people that took my sister?"

"Yes," he said.

"I did. I knew they kidnapped him and that he escaped," she said.

So, he'd kept her in the dark about his true identity as well. Mark found it a little strange that there didn't seem to be anyone Paul had ever confided in. A secret like that usually burned a person up inside until they could tell someone. Clearly, though, Paul had still feared his actual father and was willing to go to great lengths to escape him.

"You have to admit, it's a bit odd given that history that you and he…became involved," Mark said.

"You think so? Actually, he was the first person I was able to open up to. We had shared pain. It made for a lot of common ground."

"How did you meet?"

She hesitated for a moment and began fidgeting with her hands.

"He came up to me after one of my classes. He introduced himself and told me… he'd known my sister."

"Do you know why he sought you out?"

"He said he saw my picture in the student newspaper and he had to come give me his condolences."

"He told you that she was dead?" Mark asked. Sandra's body was one of the ones that had yet to be found.

"He thought so, but said he didn't know for sure."

Tears suddenly welled in her eyes. "That uncertainty…not knowing, it's what destroyed my family," she said.

"I'm sorry, I know it must be hard."

"Hard? That doesn't begin to cover it. My parents spent all their money over the years hiring private detectives, chasing down one phantom lead after another. All for nothing."

"Did they ever meet Paul? Did he tell them what he knew?"

She shook her head. "No. He didn't want to meet them. I didn't want that either. If he could have told them he knew she was dead I would have pushed, but I didn't need them taking his uncertainty for more reason to hope."

He wasn't surprised that Paul had refused to meet her parents. They might ask questions about his own "kidnapping" that he couldn't answer. The Dryer family had been just so happy to think their son was home that they had forgone asking him a lot of hard questions. The Colberts wouldn't have shown so much restraint.

"What happened with you and Paul? How did it end?"

"We were together three weeks. Such a short time and yet…" she sighed heavily. "He broke up with me. I was never really sure why. I think the connection which brought us together also proved to be too much baggage for him. His family had expectations of him and he was trying to decide what to do with his life. A couple of weeks later I had to call him with the news."

"We kept in touch all throughout the pregnancy. Probably so he could make sure I followed through on giving up the baby when it was over. There was nothing between us at that point, though. I wished there was, but…" she trailed off again.

"How would you characterize his emotional state during all of that?"

"Stressed, nervous. He was really jumpy, always looking over his shoulder like he expected to see something there."

Probably afraid the past was about to catch up with him, literally, Mark thought to himself.

"And did you have any contact with him after?"

"No. I gave up the baby and that was it."

"Which police station did you leave the baby at?" he asked.

"The one closest to campus. We both went to school at UCLA. Paul was busy trying on different graduate programs. I was still an undergrad. We went late at night, kept our faces covered in case someone saw and recognized us. He was terrified the entire time. I hated him for that. He wasn't sad, just afraid of being recognized somehow."

Mark bit his lip. He was pretty sure Paul's terror of the child falling into his real father's hands had been behind that. Why Paul hadn't moved completely out of the area once he graduated from high school Mark didn't know.

"Did you ever meet any of his friends?" Mark asked, thinking about the lawyer in Sacramento.

She shook her head. "The whole thing was quiet. It felt very forbidden. It made it exciting. I was young and stupid and didn't know better," she said bitterly.

He nodded. "Did he ever tell you anything else about why he was afraid?"

"Not directly, but when he was having his meltdown he kept repeating something over and over. I'm not sure he even realized I could hear him."

"What was it?"

She took a deep breath. "The monster is coming."

8

A chill danced up Mark's spine. "The monster is coming?"

"Yes," Sadie said.

"Do you have any idea what Paul meant by that?"

"No," she said, shaking her head. "But, he was scaring me while he was saying it."

"I don't doubt it."

Had Paul been talking about his father or something else? Either way it was ominous. Mark was only now beginning to understand how many demons his former partner had.

She had lapsed into silence, a look of pain twisting her features. An air of tragedy seemed to envelop her. He felt the sudden urge to finish as quickly as possible and get out of her way.

"The baby, did he have any distinguishing marks, birthmarks, defects, anything?"

"No, he was perfect," she murmured.

It had been a longshot.

"Did Paul ever tell you anything about the cult?" he asked.

"Only that it was hell. And that Sand…that my sister was very brave," Sadie said, her voice catching.

Mark nodded. He was pretty sure that he'd learned what he could from her and that he'd done enough damage. It was time to go.

He stood up. "Thank you for your time." He handed her a business card. "If there's anything else you can think of, I'd appreciate hearing from you," he said. "I can see myself out."

He moved to the front door and his hand was on the knob when she called after him. "Are you going to try and find him?"

"Yes, I am," he said.

He turned to look at her, but she had lapsed into silence. She was sitting, staring off into the distance at something he couldn't see. He felt a swell of pity for her. He also felt that she was beyond his help or any other person's. He saw it in his line of work. Tragedies could crush people down, grinding them into the dirt or they could provide the impetus to propel people to the heights. It was easy to see what it had done to Sadie.

He exited the house, closing the door behind him. As he walked the few steps to his car he did what he could to shrug the gloom of the place off of him. That was a burden no one should have to carry and he certainly didn't intend to take it with him.

He got in the car and pondered his options. Thirteen years ago, shortly after his birth, a baby had been abandoned at a police station in Los Angeles. Protective Services had to have a record of that and where the kid went from there. He knew a lady he could call and hopefully get some information. He pulled out his phone and called.

"Hello, this is Kendra."

"Kendra, this is Detective Mark Walters. We've spoken before."

"Of course, Detective, what can I do for you?"

"I need to find out what happened to a baby who was surrendered at a police station near UCLA thirteen years ago."

Kendra snorted. "You're a little late to the party."

"Well, better late than never."

"You have an idea of the date?"

"It would have been on or shortly after March 14th."

"Okay. Why are you trying to track down the child?"

"It's come up as part of an active investigation," Mark said. He knew Kendra, but not well enough to let her know this wasn't an official inquiry.

"Okay, I'll see what I can do."

"I appreciate it. If you could keep it confidential, that would be fantastic. We're trying to keep this as low-key as possible until we know what we're dealing with."

"I understand."

He gave her his number and she repeated it back.

"Thank you, Kendra."

"You're welcome. I'll warn you, though, this may take a couple of days. I've got several things on fire at the moment."

"Understood. I appreciate you taking the time."

He hung up. There was nothing more he could do until she came back to him with some information. Waiting was always the worst part of the job. He started the car and eased onto the road. He hoped there had been some progress from the medical examiner on the bodies. Otherwise waiting was going to be all he could do for a while.

~

"You're awfully quiet. Is something wrong?" Jeremiah asked Cindy.

They were having lunch at Rigatoni's, but she was only picking at her chicken fettucine alfredo.

"No, well, yes, but no."

"Okay, that's a confusing answer," he said.

"They're confusing emotions. Well, conflicted, at any rate."

"What is it?"

"Cartwright's fiancée came to the church this morning and confronted me."

"She what?" he asked, wondering why this was the first he was hearing of it.

"Yeah, she came in, slapped me really hard, and accused me of ruining her life basically."

Jeremiah felt himself go very still. A tight little ball of rage was forming in the pit of his stomach.

"She slapped you?" he asked. "That's why your left cheek is so red?"

"Is it?" Cindy asked, putting her hand up to it.

"Yes."

"Dang it. Oh well. At least she didn't get a chance to do it a second time. Geanie grabbed her wrist."

"Remind me to thank Geanie."

"She was raving. She's utterly convinced that Cartwright is innocent. She's sure that the police will somehow figure out that Leo killed both women."

"But Cartwright is guilty."

"I know. He confessed and everything. He tried to kill Beau. He wanted to kill me."

"Then what's wrong?"

"She was just so certain."

"She's in love with him. If she weren't in denial then she'd have to deal with the fact that she nearly married him without knowing what he had done and what he was capable of. She probably can't cope with that, so she's sold herself a fairy tale about him being innocent."

"I guess the thing is that she reminded me of myself."

"How?" Jeremiah asked.

"When we were on the cattle drive and the evidence seemed to be pointing to you I was adamant that you were innocent. I was just as passionate about your innocence as she is about Cartwright's."

"Just because someone is passionate about something doesn't make it true."

"I know, but I still keep going over it in my head. There's no way to mistake his admission or his intention to hurt me. No, he absolutely confessed to killing Rose. That wasn't me putting words in his mouth or mistaking his meaning."

He reached out and took her hand. A little jolt of electricity went through him. Public displays of affection were still new for them and they still made him feel a bit giddy and trepidacious all at the same time.

"Cartwright killed Rose. End of story. This woman is a grieving bride. You and she have nothing in common."

Cindy chuckled ruefully. "You're right. She's one hundred percent convinced that Cartwright is innocent. I wasn't that sure you were."

"Really?"

She nodded.

"You thought I might be behind the murders on the cattle drive?"

"I didn't think you were. I also didn't put it past you. I knew you were quite capable of it. I also knew that if you did you had to have a good reason."

He rubbed the back of her hand with his thumb. "And yet, sitting in the back of that chuck wagon, you agreed to run away with me anyway."

"Did I?" Cindy asked, blushing.

"Uh huh."

"Well, it was very indecent of you to suggest it, especially since you knew you were innocent and you and Mark had cooked up the whole scheme." She met his eyes. Hers were quickening with thought. "Did you…were you testing me? My feelings for you?" she asked.

"Maybe in a way I was. Mostly I was caught up in the moment. Lost in the part. And besides, I've wanted to ask you to run away with me every day since the day we met."

It was true, part of him had yearned for that all along even though he hadn't allowed himself to think about it for more than a second.

She blushed harder. It was so cute when she did that. He squeezed her hand.

"It took you long enough," she said.

He grinned. "I know. I'm an idiot for that. And this woman's an idiot for refusing to see the truth."

"You're right. A very angry idiot. Now, if you'll excuse me for a moment."

Cindy got up and he turned his head so he could watch her as she walked to the restroom. Around them other diners were enjoying their lunch. A waitress was serving heaping plates of pasta to a table three over from theirs. He could hear the tinkle of the bells above the front door as someone opened it.

When Cindy had disappeared from view he turned back around and then froze. In the middle of the table, between her plate and his, was a knife that had not been there a moment before.

He swept the room with his eyes as his heart began to beat faster. No one was looking his way. He got up and made his way swiftly to the front door. He yanked it open and looked up and down the sidewalk. There were a couple of people walking leisurely by but that was it.

He turned and surveyed the restaurant again. Someone had managed to put that knife on the table while his back was turned. That was no easy task.

He walked slowly back to his chair, grappling with his emotions. By the time she returned to the table he had moved the knife and was wearing a fake smile.

"Where were we?" Cindy asked brightly as she sat back down.

"We were talking about the psycho lady. You know, I can teach you how to block it if someone tries to slap you again," he said, trying to sound casual as he dropped his eyes back to his meal.

"It's the first time someone's slapped me other than my brother when we were kids. I don't anticipate it happening again."

"Well, you know, I could always show you just in case."

"Are you offering to teach me self-defense?" she asked.

"Yes."

"Why now?"

"Well, you just got slapped."

"I've been in danger loads of times, had guns pointed at me, been tied up, and now you're suggesting it over a slap? That doesn't make sense. What's the real reason?"

He grimaced. That hadn't taken her long to figure out. She was becoming a better sleuth every day. Either that or she was just becoming more suspicious and used to looking for people's ulterior motives. Either way it was impressive.

No one in the restaurant seemed to be paying any attention to him. Still, it was not a conversation he wanted to have in public. "I saw the traveling medical supplies salesman today. You know, the one you first met in Vegas?"

"Martin?" she asked, eyes growing wide.

He nodded.

"What was he doing here?" she asked.

"His job, but he made a point of saying hello."

"Why?"

He lowered his voice. "I can explain more later. He did let me know that someone might be coming after me in the near future."

She blanched. "Oh," was all she said.

"So, it wouldn't be a bad idea for you to learn some self-defense basics. Frankly, I should have taught you years ago. I just didn't like the idea of you having to worry about that kind of stuff."

"There are times when it would have come in handy. Better to know and not need it ever again than to need it and not know it," she said.

"You're right, of course."

"When do we start?"

"We might as well get on with it. We can start tonight after work."

She nodded resolutely. "That works for me. I think this is a good idea. I'm glad you had it."

He smiled at her. She was right, better to be overprepared than underprepared. As for him, he didn't want to wait for someone to maybe come find him. It was time to go on the offensive.

~

Mark decided to cut right to the chase. He went to see the coroner. Harry was the one who had called Mark and told him that the bones of the real Paul Dryer had been found in the mass grave at Green Pastures. Ever since then he'd never been able to look at the man the same way. Sure, he'd only been the messenger, but the message had been profoundly disturbing and had sent him on the crazy quest he'd been on for so long now.

"How you doing, Detective?" Harry asked.

"Okay, and you?"

"Can't complain. Course, if I did, who would listen?" Harry said with a smile.

The man had a morbid sense of humor that Mark was pretty sure came with the job.

"Find anything I should know about?" Mark asked.

"Always. First off, you should know that a young fellow named Beau positively identified Miss Meyer earlier."

Mark nodded.

"Poor guy was pretty broken up about it, too. Wasn't much I could say to make him feel better."

"There usually isn't. I'm sorry, Harry, I should have been here to handle that."

"Not a problem. It's good for me to talk to someone who hasn't been corpsified every now and then."

"I would imagine so."

"You talk to the dead all day long and after a while you realize you can't remember how to talk to the living."

"So, you talk to them differently?" Mark asked against his better judgment.

"Of course," Harry said, looking at him like he was crazy. "You don't expect the one type to answer you back."

The way he said it, the crazy roll of his eyes, and Harry could have easily been talking about either group.

"What else can you tell me?" Mark asked.

"Victim was indeed pregnant, as suspected. I also discovered that she was killed a couple of weeks ago and that our other victim was killed maybe three or four days later."

"Okay, what else?"

Harry got a sly smile on his face. "There is one really fascinating thing I discovered, a link, you might say, between the two victims."

"Oh?" Mark asked, standing straighter.

Harry nodded and turned to face Mark head on. He had a gloating smile; clearly he thought he'd found something truly worthwhile.

"Are you ready for this?"

"Yes," Mark said.

"Both victims were killed the exact same way, strangled to death."

9

Mark stared intently at Harry. "Was it the same killer?" he asked.

Harry shrugged. "That I can't tell you. We were able to lift prints off the one woman, but there were no prints at all on Rose."

Mark sighed in frustration. "Is there anything else you can tell me?"

"I think April was unconscious when she was strangled."

"And Rose?"

Harry shook his head. "I'm pretty sure based on what I've seen that she was awake and put up a struggle."

"Okay, thanks. Let me know if you come up with anything else."

"Don't I always?"

"Yup."

Mark left. He was feeling antsy. There was something wrong about all of this. He had no doubt about Cartwright's guilt, at least when it came to Rose. Leo, however, was a big question mark. One that he needed to spend some time with.

A few minutes later Mark was sitting down in an interrogation room across the table from Leo. The man looked rough and Mark was certain he hadn't slept at all since he'd been arrested. He might break now if pushed, but Mark thought about Cindy. This guy had spent his only call on her and she believed him innocent.

"How are you doing?" he asked.

"How do you think?" the man asked, the distress clear in his voice. He was on the verge of hysteria which could be good if he was guilty but would be decidedly unhelpful if he was innocent.

"Would you like some coffee?" Mark asked.

Leo nodded.

"Okay, I'll be right back."

Mark returned a minute later with coffee for both of them and half a box of donuts he'd found in the break room. He set them down. Leo all but lunged at the box. He grabbed a chocolate frosted and began devouring it like a starving man. Even though he should have been offered meals it was likely he'd been unwilling or unable to eat before now. It was amazing what a box of comfort food could do for a man's outlook.

Leo was halfway through his second donut before he looked up at Mark, making eye contact for the first time. He saw fear and confusion there but no traces of guilt. Either the guy was in complete denial or Mark was inclined to believe that he was innocent despite the physical evidence.

"So, tell me about Cartwright's bachelor party," Mark said as he retrieved a donut for himself.

"I don't remember very much of it," Leo said.

"Why not? One too many to drink?"

"I don't know. I only had two beers which is my normal limit."

Mark raised an eyebrow. "Two beers and you don't remember the rest of the night? Were they yard-longs or something?"

"No, normal size."

"Sounds like some strong brew. I need to get some of that for the next time my mother-in-law's in town, you know what I mean?" Mark asked with a grin.

Leo just shook his head. "Trust me, the hangover was so not worth it."

"Can you tell me who else was there?"

Leo scrunched up his forehead like he was thinking. "Cartwright, of course, and his best man, Ivan. He's the one who invited me. I think I was introduced to a cousin. Then there were two other guys from work. Lloyd, he's an accountant and Gareth who's in sales. I tell you, he and Ivan got along like a house on fire. They kept whispering and laughing. I think someone at one point told them to get a room."

"Ivan and Gareth are gay?" Mark asked.

"I didn't think Gareth was, but I don't really know him all that well. Ivan, I have no clue."

"Do you remember anyone else from the party?"

"There might have been one other guy, and if anyone came late I don't remember them."

"You said Ivan invited you?"

"Yeah, it was a bit of a surprise. I guess he had to scrape the bottom of the barrel to find people who wanted to attend Cartwright's party."

"Why did you go?" Mark asked.

"He's technically my boss. I didn't exactly feel like I could refuse."

That made sense. What didn't make sense was that Leo reluctantly went to a bachelor party, had two beers and got so wasted he killed a stripper and didn't remember it. There was something very wrong about the whole thing. He was inclined to agree with Cindy that Leo was innocent even though things looked bad for him.

"How did Ivan contact you?"

"He called me. I guess Cartwright gave him my number although he must have gone into my HR files to get it."

"Do you still have Ivan's contact information?"

Leo frowned. "Yeah, it should be in my phone. I saved it in case I needed it."

"Great, I'll get that from you in a few minutes."

"I don't have my phone. The officers took it."

"I know," Mark said quickly, not wanting him to get sidetracked. "What else can you tell me about Ivan?"

"He and Cartwright went to college together. Neither of them is exactly…nice. He seemed like a snob and a jerk. You know the type, thinks that anyone who didn't go to an ivy league school is beneath them."

"I've met a couple of those," Mark admitted. "Always loads of fun, particularly at parties. You said there was a cousin maybe, what was he like?"

Leo shook his head. "I didn't really interact with him. At least, not that I remember."

Mark realized he wasn't going to get much more out of Leo, at least, not at that point. What he needed was to reach out to Ivan and talk to him about the party and what he knew of the stripper.

He wrapped up with Leo and fifteen minutes later got what he needed off the man's phone. He made his way to his desk and got comfortable before calling Ivan. His cell had an east coast area code. It rang twice and then a deep male voice answered.

"Go for Ivan."

"Hello, Ivan, my name is Detective Mark Walters, I'm with the Pine Springs Police Department. How are you today?"

There was a pause and when the man spoke again his voice was decidedly frosty. "I'd be a lot better if some Neanderthal in your department hadn't wrongfully accused my best friend of murder."

"The reason I'm calling today is related to that," Mark said, ignoring the jab. It wouldn't do to trade barbs with the man. "Are you familiar with a Miss April Snow?"

"I don't think…wait a minute, that sounds like the name of the…ah…entertainer I hired for Kenneth's bachelor party. At least, it sounds similar."

It sounded like he then covered the phone and was speaking with someone else.

"So, you were the one who hired her," Mark said.

"What?" Ivan asked. "You've called at a bad time. I'm in the middle of getting fitted for a tux."

"Here in town?" Mark asked.

"Yeah," Ivan responded, clearly distracted.

"That's okay. I can come to you. It will be easier that way," Mark said.

Ten minutes later he was having the weirdest sense of déjà vu as he walked into the tuxedo shop that Jeremiah and Joseph had once been poisoned in. It must have been a slow afternoon because when Mark walked in there only seemed to be two men present. One was tall and slender and wearing a tuxedo. The other was short and stooped over as he pinned the hems.

"Ivan?" Mark asked as he moved into the man's line of sight.

"That's me. You must be the detective," Ivan said with a grimace.

Mark plastered his best fake smile on while secretly hoping that the man in front of him was his perpetrator so he could lock him up and throw away the key.

"I am," Mark said, swallowing down a sarcastic response.

"Well, then, what's this all about? What does the stripper have to do with Kenneth?" Ivan asked, managing to sound supremely bored.

"Well, for one, like his mistress she's turned up dead," Mark said.

Ivan looked at him sharply. "She's dead?" he asked.

Either the man was surprised or he was a studied liar. Mark wasn't ruling out either at that moment.

"Very much so. It looks like she was killed the night of the party."

"That's…extraordinary. What incredibly unfortunate timing."

"I'd call it a little more than unfortunate," Mark said, unable to keep the sarcasm out of his voice this time. He pulled his notepad and pen out of his pocket. "How did you hire her?" he asked.

"Through a service. Sight unseen, I'm afraid. I live in New York so I had to plan the party remotely."

"Party's been over a couple of weeks. What are you still doing out here?" Mark asked.

Ivan glared at him. "I stuck around a little longer to try and help my friend out, prove his innocence. That and I had several business meetings that I was able to arrange so I plan to be here for at least a few more days."

"Must be some big shindig coming up for you to be getting the tux," Mark noted.

"I'm attending a very prestigious gala on Friday night."

"Why not just wear whatever you were planning on wearing to Kenneth's wedding?" Mark asked.

Ivan looked at him like he was a moron. "Kenneth's wedding was only black tie. This is white tie. You understand, of course," he said in a tone that indicated that he clearly expected Mark not to.

He tried not to bristle at the other man's dismissive manner. One of the most important things you learned as a detective was to take control of the conversation and keep it on your terms.

"So, we know that Kenneth killed his girlfriend because she was pregnant and he didn't want her screwing up his wedding. Why did he kill the stripper?" Mark asked.

"I beg your pardon. He most certainly did not kill the stripper."

"Oh?"

"Or that other girl," Ivan hastily added.

"That's not what it's going to look like to a jury," Mark said. "It's pretty clear he killed both of them."

"That's impossible! I was with him the entire time at the party. The stripper left at two in the morning and we didn't call it a night until four."

"So, what, you're suggesting someone else at the party killed the stripper? Okay, tell me who and I won't have Kenneth charged with her murder as well."

"What you're suggesting is preposterous. I have no idea where the young lady went after she left."

"How do you know she left?" Mark pressed.

"Because I paid her and then she disappeared. Ergo, she left."

"Or she was busy being murdered. I hear Kenneth's cousin has quite the temper. Maybe he did her in."

Ivan actually burst out laughing. "Reginald? Reginald is so fat and weak there's no way he could even contemplate something that would take as much energy as killing a woman. The man practically has a heart attack just trying to walk across the room."

Mark would have to check out Reginald, but if what Ivan said was true he could probably rule him out as a suspect. At least his fishing expedition worked and Ivan had given him some kind of information.

"What about Gareth? Did he even look at April or was he too busy hitting on you all night?" Mark asked.

"What?" Ivan demanded, jerking slightly and turning red in the face.

The tailor must have stabbed him when he moved because Ivan jerked again and turned his wrath on the poor man. "You clumsy idiot! You stabbed me."

"I'm sorry, sir," the man muttered.

For just a moment Mark allowed himself to hope that the needle was poisoned. He shook himself. He shouldn't think like that. The guy was getting under his skin, though.

"I heard that Gareth was all over you and that you weren't exactly rebuffing him," Mark said, intentionally exaggerating what Leo had told him.

"Whoever said so was a liar!"

"You know, it's okay to admit-"

"We were talking business," Ivan snapped.

"If you say so," Mark said, giving him a wink.

"He wants to join my…golf club. That's what we were discussing if you must know," Ivan said, clearly angry.

Mark barely managed to suppress a smile. It was clear with Ivan that image was everything. Pushing his buttons in that area had worked. It had worked so well that Ivan almost gave something up. Whatever Gareth was interested in joining, Mark was pretty sure it wasn't a golf club.

"Whatever, it's no skin off my nose. I'm going to see him next and I can tell him you said 'hi'," Mark said.

He expected Ivan to have another outburst. Instead the man turned pale. "You'll do no such thing," he hissed quietly.

"Then tell me why the two of you were plotting to kill April," Mark said.

Something changed in Ivan's eyes. It was as if the man coiled back in on himself like a snake. "We're done here," he said in clipped tones.

"We're done when I say we are," Mark countered, putting an edge into his voice. "Tell me who killed her and maybe I won't arrest you as an accessory to murder."

Ivan smiled. "I have no idea who killed her, and you can't arrest a man for throwing a party."

"I wouldn't be so sure about that," Mark said, intentionally smiling at the man in what he hoped was an intimidating fashion. He turned and strode for the door.

"Oh, Detective, if you're looking for someone to pin this murder on, try a fellow named Leo who works with Kenneth. He couldn't keep his eyes off April all night."

Mark didn't answer. A minute later he was in his car. The one thing he'd learned from the encounter was that he was pretty sure Ivan knew something about what had happened to April. He purposely hadn't mentioned any details, such as the fact that she had been strangled, because he was hoping to get him or his compatriot to slip up later.

It was almost five by the time he got back to his desk. There was a nagging feeling in the back of his head like he was forgetting something. Try as he might, though, he couldn't put his finger on it.

Twenty minutes effort was all it took to confirm that Cartwright's cousin, Reginald, was in as poor a condition as Ivan had made it out. Mark certainly didn't see him strangling anyone to death. He hadn't managed to find out from Ivan if there had been anyone at the party that he didn't already know about. He wasn't sure how forthcoming the man would have been on that topic.

Instead he would visit Cartwright and put some pressure on him. Being charged with two murders was worse than one. He might just be eager to turn over on someone, hoping that it would shed doubt on his own guilt. That was, if he didn't kill April as well as Rose.

He'd go pay him a visit in the morning and see what he could pry out of the man. That left talking to Gareth. He should also pay a visit to Reginald just to see if the man knew anything or had seen anything. Same thing with Lloyd.

Ironically, Ivan's parting shot about Leo had made Mark feel even more certain that the man wasn't their killer. His fingerprints on April's neck were enough to charge him, but Mark didn't want to charge a potentially innocent man if he didn't have to. They couldn't keep him much longer without charging him, though.

Ultimately, with the blessing of his captain, Mark read Leo the riot act about not leaving town and let him go. He also tasked a couple of uniforms with watching him for the next forty-eight hours until he knew more one way or another.

Leo was so relieved to go that he began to cry. Mark felt for him and the ordeal he'd gone through. Once everything had been taken care of he glanced at the clock and noticed it was now after six.

Mark still had a feeling he was forgetting something as he headed home. As he drove he kept going over and over in his mind the conversation with Ivan. It was going to be interesting to see how Gareth responded to the same insinuations. Mark had a feeling there was something the two men were hiding. He just didn't know yet what it was.

He finally pulled into the driveway. He got out of the car and headed to the front door. His shoulder was beginning to really ache again. He'd grab some painkillers and hopefully they'd kick in during dinner. He held out his key, and just before he could insert it in the lock, the door flew open. A man was standing there glowering at him.

10

As startled as he was it took Mark a moment to recognize Joseph standing there. Geanie appeared over his shoulder a moment later.

"Joseph, Geanie! What are you two doing here?" Mark asked.

Geanie arched an eyebrow. "We're here to babysit while you two go on date night," she said.

Mark cringed inside. He had completely forgotten. "How mad is she?"

"Not half as mad as we're going to be if the two of you don't get out of here and have some fun," Joseph said, standing aside to let him enter.

"She knows you're here. She's putting the babies down and will be out here in ten minutes or less," Geanie said.

Joseph and Geanie genuinely seemed to like babysitting, which was a blessing for Mark and Traci. What was even better is that they were far more trustworthy than a babysitter. Not to mention cheaper. They always did it for nothing. After all, it wasn't like they needed the money.

A sudden thought occurred to Mark. Not only was Joseph wealthy, but he was also from old money. There was just a tiny shot he would have heard something about the bank where Paul had kept the birth certificate.

"Joseph, have you ever heard of the Five Diamond Bank?"

"In Sacramento? Yes. Frankly, I'm surprised you have."

"Do you have a box there?"

"Why?" Joseph asked, eyes narrowing slightly.

Mark was a bit surprised. The other man was usually the most open person he knew. The fact that he didn't answer straight out was odd, to say the least. He cleared his throat. "I'm trying to figure out a few things. If you had a box at the bank, what kind of items would you keep there?"

Joseph cleared his throat as well. "Theoretically?"

"Theoretically," Mark affirmed.

"Well, something incredibly valuable, priceless even. Or, again, theoretically, enough cash to disappear if there was ever a need."

Mark just stared at Joseph, struggling to come up with a response. Finally, he blurted out, "How much cash would that be?"

"More than enough," Joseph said.

"Why? I mean, very few people would ever have need of such a thing."

"I was a Boy Scout," Joseph said. "There was one invaluable lesson I learned from that experience."

"Be prepared?" Mark guessed.

"Be prepared."

Joseph paused and glanced at Geanie then turned back to Mark. "Why do you want to know about that bank?"

Mark grimaced. "I had an unfortunate run in there on Monday. I learned the hard way that the bankers there are serious about security."

"Deadly serious," Joseph said with a straight face.

"Tell me about it," Mark said, rubbing his shoulder. "I'm surprised that place is still operating."

Joseph actually gave him a pitying look. "Mark, I think you'd be shocked at the institutions that exist in this country, the things that can be done or acquired, if you know the right people or have the right…credentials."

"Credentials. Being a billionaire like you, you mean?"

Joseph nodded and Mark felt himself reeling. He'd said "billionaire" expecting Joseph to contradict him. He hadn't. Everyone knew that Joseph was incredibly rich, but in that moment Mark had an inkling that none of them really knew just how rich the man was.

"I'm starting to get an idea," Mark said.

"You'll forgive my curiosity, but why were you there?" Joseph asked.

"It turns out the key that Paul left his ex-wife went to a safety deposit box there."

It was Joseph's turn to be clearly startled. "Did you find out what was in it?"

"A birth certificate. It turns out that Paul had a son."

"What?" Joseph and Geanie chorused.

"Yeah."

"Why would someone go to all those lengths to hide that?" Geanie asked.

"Those are extreme measures to take," Joseph added.

"All I can think of is he was afraid of someone finding out. It makes me wonder if he was concerned about his real father discovering that he had a grandchild."

"Things with him just keep getting more and more disturbing," Joseph noted.

"Some days I think it will never be over," Mark admitted.

"I can imagine," the other man said with a sympathetic look. "It must be rough."

Before Mark could respond Traci came walking in from the other room. She looked stunning in a royal blue dress. She had her hair up and he relaxed when she smiled at him. It was her happy smile and not her I'm-going-to-kill-you smile.

He moved forward and gave her a lingering kiss. "You look breathtaking," he said.

"Do you like my new dress?"

"I love it,"

"Good," she said. "And, you can afford it."

"Even better," he said with a grin. He offered her his arm. "Shall we go?"

She giggled like a school girl and the rest of the world seemed to fade away.

~

Cindy and Jeremiah were in the middle of eating Chinese take-out when her phone rang. She was surprised when she answered to hear Leo on the other end.

"Leo, are you okay?" she asked anxiously.

"They let me go. Detective Mark warned me not to leave town. I'm still a suspect and everything."

"But at least you're not being held anymore. That's a very good sign and it has to be a huge relief."

"It is and I know I owe it all to you. Thank you."

"I didn't do that much," she said.

"No, you did everything. I can never repay you, really."

"You're welcome. So, are you heading home?"

"I guess. To be honest, I'm exhausted and I don't really know what to do with myself. I should probably stop off first and get something to eat somewhere," he said, sounding completely lost.

She frowned. "Mark said you were still a suspect?"

"Yes."

"Did he say who else is a suspect at this point?"

"No."

Cindy glanced at Jeremiah. "Can you hold on for a second, Leo?" she asked.

"Sure."

She covered the phone with her hand and quickly told Jeremiah what was going on. He raised an eyebrow.

"You want to invite him over here, don't you?" he asked.

"Is it a bad idea?" she asked, wincing slightly.

He shook his head. "Go ahead. I'll put the fear of God in him if need be."

"Thank you," she said. She brought the phone back up. "Leo, we're having Chinese food at my house if you want to come over and discuss your case more."

There was a pause and then he said, "I wouldn't want to impose like that."

"It's fine, really. We need to talk anyway and the food's already here."

"That would be great," he said, the relief in his voice evident.

She gave him her address and then hung up.

"Was that a stupid idea?" she asked Jeremiah.

"I would have waited and had lunch with him tomorrow, someplace public just to be on the safe side, but I understand the impulse. You're a very compassionate woman," he said, smiling at her.

"Thanks. After he goes tonight, though, I'm going to really want some of those self-defense lessons."

"You'll get them," he promised.

She went to the kitchen and got an extra plate and set of chopsticks. She briefly debated calling Mark but decided to talk to him after she'd had a chance to talk with Leo. Clearly Mark wasn't convinced of his guilt or Leo wouldn't be free.

A few minutes later the doorbell rang and she hurried to open the door.

"Hi," Leo said sheepishly. He walked in looking like the living dead. He was wearing the same clothes she'd seen him in at the precinct the day before. It was evidence that he had come straight to her house instead of stopping off at home.

"Hi, come in."

He followed her inside and she set him up with a plate of food which he began to eat hungrily.

"You look exhausted," Cindy noted.

"I am. I haven't slept," he said. "I keep hoping that tomorrow when I wake up that this will all have just been some crazy nightmare."

"I'm so sorry. I know what it's like to go through a traumatic experience."

"I kind of had that impression. That, and the way you solved Rose's murder, was why I called you. Thank you again for coming down yesterday, for believing me. Honestly, I couldn't think of anyone else I could turn to in that moment. Which, given that we worked together for all of three days, has me seriously reevaluating my life at the moment."

Her pity for him deepened. There was a time when she'd avoided getting too close to people, afraid of getting hurt. Now, though, she had a circle of friends that she couldn't imagine living without. They were what helped her get through the hard times and were there to celebrate the good times.

"It's natural to do a lot of soul searching after something terrible and unexpected happens," Jeremiah said.

"I'm figuring that out. What I can't figure out still is why I can't remember most of the night of the bachelor party," he said. "Detective Mark asked me a lot about the party, too, and I just can't remember."

Cindy glanced at Jeremiah whose brow was furrowed in thought. "You only had two drinks, right?" he asked.

"Yes."

"Did you make it through the second one?"

"I…you know I can't really remember," Leo said. "How pathetic is that?"

"Not pathetic. I think that perhaps someone slipped something into your drink so that you wouldn't remember," Jeremiah said.

"What do you mean? Like a roofie?" Leo asked, sounding a bit bewildered.

Cindy nodded. That actually made a lot more sense. If the real killer slipped something in his drink then the rest of the night would be a total blur to him.

"How did you get home that night?" she asked.

"Someone must have driven me. Ivan had us all picked up in a limo for the party. I'm guessing that's how I got home."

Cindy exchanged glances with Jeremiah. Mark should be able to find out what limo company Ivan used. Then hopefully the driver noticed something about Leo when he took him home.

"I still don't understand, why would someone put something in my drink?" Leo asked.

"So that you wouldn't remember what happened, what you did, what they framed you for," Cindy said.

More than ever she was convinced that Leo had to be innocent. She remembered how terrible he'd looked the morning after the party. Either he was lying or mistaken about how much he'd had to drink or there had been something else at play.

Leo suddenly turned pale. "You don't think they spiked my drink by accident, do you?"

"What do you mean?" Cindy asked.

"What if they were trying to roofie that poor girl instead?"

"We don't actually know that they didn't roofie her," Cindy said. "I doubt if she was working the party, though, that she would have been drinking. I mean, that just seems really reckless. Then again, I wouldn't know," she ended with a frustrated sigh.

"Let's assume you were the target," Jeremiah said. "I mean, it's pretty easy to frame a man for murder when he himself has to admit he has no memory of the events."

"But who would want to kill that girl? And frame me?" Leo asked, the distress heavy in his voice.

"That's what we need to find out," Cindy said. "The beginning of the evening, do you remember anyone acting strange, like nervous or anxious?"

"Gareth was really keyed up, but then I think he was hitting on Ivan. The two of them kept kind of huddling together, whispering. At least, I remember that they were."

"Who is Gareth?" Cindy asked.

"He's a salesman who works at Rayburn. You probably didn't get a chance to meet him. He's intense, the type to always win salesman of the year."

"What else do you know about him?" Jeremiah asked.

"He's ambitious. He must be a really good salesman, too. Last year he bought himself a Ferrari. I think he made everyone in the building go see it. Wouldn't let any of us sit in it, though, except for Kenneth. Frankly if he's as good as he thinks he is I'm surprised he hasn't moved on to an even bigger company."

"Kenneth seemed ambitious, too, but he didn't need to jump to another company since he was marrying the owner's daughter," Cindy mused.

"Yeah. I always had a feeling that was just a first stepping stone for him, though."

Cindy thought about her run-in with Kenneth's former fiancée. "Have you ever met Nita Rayburn?"

"A couple of times. Seen her around more than that," Leo said, before shoveling some more food into his mouth.

"What's your take on her?"

"Spoiled, entitled, and yet, somehow, wildly naïve. You'd think a woman like her could have sniffed out a man like Kenneth's true intentions from the start. She didn't, though."

"Well, they say love is blind," Jeremiah said.

"I guess. Maybe she's just so self-centered she assumed that he had to love her for her. I don't know."

"Who else was at the party?" Cindy asked.

"Lloyd from accounting."

"What do you know about him?"

Leo shrugged. "He's an accountant, not much more to know than that. Unless there are numbers involved he's not interested."

"Okay, who else?"

"Kenneth's cousin. The man seemed like his polar opposite in every way. Then, of course, there was Ivan who planned the whole thing."

"So, five men besides you?"

"As far as I know. Is that important?"

Cindy nodded. "Unless I'm wrong, one of those five men roofied you, killed April, and framed you for it. The only question is, which one?"

Leo turned noticeably paler. "Which one of them did this to me?"

She nodded.

He shook his head. "The cousin doesn't even know me and I don't see him being able to pull all that off."

"That leaves Ivan, Kenneth, Gareth, and Lloyd," Jeremiah said.

"Kenneth killed Rose. Doesn't it make sense that he would kill April?" Leo asked.

"Not necessarily. He had a reason for killing Rose. It was an awful reason, but it fit in line with his ambitions. What possible motive could he have for killing April?" Cindy asked.

"I don't-"

There was a sudden pounding on the front door. "Open up! Police!"

Cindy jerked in her chair, but before she could move the window in the kitchen exploded inward in a hail of glass, and a metal canister landed at her feet.

11

Gas erupted out of the canister. Before Cindy could move Jeremiah lunged to his feet. He grabbed the canister and heaved it back out the window it had come from.

"We are unarmed!" he shouted at the top of his lungs.

His mind raced. Something had gone horribly wrong. He had no idea if it was the actual police outside or someone else. Either way they could be in serious trouble. He'd hidden weapons in Cindy's house where she was unlikely to find them. Going for one now, though, could prove fatal if it really was the police who were raiding them.

Suddenly he heard a shot ring out. He tackled Cindy to the ground and covered her body with his own. He looked up at Leo. "Get down!" he screamed at him.

Leo was gaping, clearly in shock. Jeremiah moved slightly, reaching out to pull him off the chair when the front door exploded inward. A moment later bullets hit Leo. He fell off the chair, landing next to Cindy who began to scream as his blood sprayed on her.

Jeremiah covered Cindy's head and torso with his own body, elevating his hands into the air to show he held no weapon. He prayed as fast and as hard as he could in that moment as he watched black uniformed SWAT members pour into Cindy's living room.

He didn't know why they were there but he just prayed they didn't try to shoot Cindy and him, too. He risked a glance at Leo. The man was dead. He'd taken two shots to the chest and one to the head.

Booted feet ran through the house while two men trained their guns on him. He heard shouts of "Clear!" going up all around.

"Cindy, quiet," he whispered to her.

She stopped screaming. The sound would have kept the men aiming weapons at them more tense and jumpy. He could hear a quiet sniffle and then she fell completely silent. He could feel the terror in her body. In that moment it matched his. He couldn't lose her. Not now. Not like this.

The gun he usually wore on him he always left in the car when he came into her house, not wanting her to hug him and find it on him. That was probably a very good thing at the moment even though he wished he had it with him.

There were more running bootsteps and then the SWAT members seemed to have all gathered back in the living room.

"Name!" one of them barked at him.

"Rabbi Jeremiah Silverman and Cindy Preston. We are friends of Detectives Mark Walters and Liam O'Neill. Call them, please."

"Rabbi? You okay?"

The crowd parted and he saw a uniformed officer standing in the doorway. He'd met the man before and his mind frantically searched for the name. "Francis! No, we're not okay. Could you please get these guys to stop aiming guns at us?"

"Hey, this is the rabbi and the church secretary. You guys are here to rescue them," Francis said sharply.

"You can positively identify them?" the leader of the SWAT team asked.

"Of course I can."

There was a terrible moment of silence and then the SWAT leader looked around. "Stand down."

Weapons were holstered or at least lowered. Jeremiah heaved a sigh of relief. Francis pushed his way through the crowd and crouched down next to them, his face filled with concern. "They didn't hit you did they?" he asked, seeing all the blood.

"I don't think so," Jeremiah said.

Francis reached for his radio and quickly called for an ambulance. "It's going to be okay," he told him once he had.

"Can you call Mark?" Jeremiah asked.

Francis nodded. "Yes, I will. Right away."

Jeremiah nodded. Underneath him Cindy was beginning to shake. She was going into shock. She had seen death before, up close. She had seen him kill bad guys right in front of her. This was different, though. Leo wasn't a bad guy. He was a friend she was trying to help, and the police had gunned him down in her house right in front of her.

He had to find out why. She wasn't going to be okay until they could make sense of all of this. But he wasn't moving or doing anything else until he was one hundred percent sure it was safe to do so. Unfortunately, that meant she was stuck on the floor face-to-face with a dead man.

"Close your eyes, darling," he whispered to her. "I've got you."

A shudder passed through her and he could feel her hands plucking at his shirt.

"I've got you," he said again.

He kept repeating it over and over until he could hear the sound of sirens. Strangely he was reminded of their first meeting when he'd held her on the floor of the church sanctuary while a dead man lay on the floor nearby. He had held her and listened to the sound of the sirens, trying to reassure her that everything would be okay. Violence had invaded her church, her sanctuary, literally. Now violence had invaded her home which should have been a sanctuary.

The difference this time was that she wasn't a stranger. She was the woman he loved, and he would do anything to take this pain from her.

The paramedics arrived. They were quick to cover the body with a sheet which he appreciated. Then they turned to Cindy and him.

"Are you hurt?" the one asked, bending down so he was eye-level with Jeremiah.

"I don't think so," he answered.

"What about her?"

"She's gone into shock."

"Can you get up so I can examine her?"

He knew he had to, but he didn't want to. Part of him was afraid that if he did the SWAT team members that he could still see would suddenly pull their guns on her.

"Cindy, I'm going to get up so the paramedic can look at you," Jeremiah said.

"No," she sobbed.

The sound tore at him.

"They need to make sure you aren't hurt."

"No, if you get up something bad will happen. They'll kill you. They'll kill us."

She was hysterical, but she was giving voice to his own fears. He struggled with what to do. Then, suddenly, a voice he recognized cut through the chatter around them.

"All of you officers clear the hell out of here right now!"

He looked up. Mark was standing in the doorway, features twisted in a snarl.

"Sir-" one of the officers started to say.

"Out. Now. Or so help me God I will put an end to your career and your life."

He had never seen Mark look that frightening or use that tone of voice, not even on criminals. It had an impact because the police who were standing around all hurried past him. Once the last one was outside Mark slammed the door which was sagging on its hinges and came swiftly toward them.

He dropped onto his knees beside them. "What have those bastards done?" he whispered, voice filling with horror.

"Cindy, Mark's here, he sent all the others away. It's just him and us and the paramedics. You have to let them look at you now," he said.

"It hurts so bad," she moaned, her breath catching in her throat.

Terror knifed through him. Had she been hit and he hadn't realized it?

"Darling, I'm getting up now. I promise you, it's going to be okay," he said, hearing his own voice crack.

He didn't know how long he'd been laying on top of her, but he suddenly discovered that his muscles had locked up. Fortunately, Mark reached out and helped him push up and then roll off of Cindy as gently as he could.

She lay curled on the floor, eyes wide, pupils dilated. He didn't see any bullet wounds but he did suddenly notice the way in which she was holding her arm. He felt sick inside as he realized it was likely broken.

He sat up and Mark put an arm behind his back. "I've got you," he said.

A paramedic handed Mark a blanket and he slung it around Jeremiah.

The paramedics were moving their hands over Cindy gingerly, checking for injury. When they got to her right arm she screamed.

"Ma'am, can you move the arm?" the one asked.

She tried and it made a jerking motion as she did. Jeremiah felt the knife twist in his gut.

"It looks broken," the other paramedic said.

"It must have happened when I tackled her to the floor," Jeremiah said.

"Probably saved her life doing it."

"We're going to have to take you to the hospital for some x-rays," one of the men said to Cindy.

She looked up at Jeremiah, her eyes still wide in terror.

He forced himself to smile even though it was the last thing in the world he felt like doing. "It's okay. I'll go with you."

"My arm hurts," she whimpered.

"I know, sweetie, I know," he said. He glanced up at the paramedics. "Can you give her something for the pain?"

One nodded. "Once we get her into the ambulance I can give her some morphine."

"Then let's get moving," Jeremiah growled.

"We'll grab the stretcher and be right back. I don't want to move her any more than we have to until she gets some tests," he said, standing up.

The two men moved swiftly toward the front door.

"What happened, Mark?" Jeremiah asked.

"I don't know. I was at dinner with Traci when Francis called and said SWAT had killed Leo in Cindy's house."

"I was here when it happened. There was no provocation. They didn't even give us a chance to say anything. He wasn't armed. They just broke down the door, came in and shot him. I'm pretty sure if we hadn't hit the floor they would have shot us, too."

Mark shook his head looking ashen. "None of it makes sense. Francis and his partner were supposed to be keeping an eye on Leo. They were up the street in a patrol car when SWAT showed up. They didn't explain anything to them or give them time to object from my understanding."

"Something is seriously wrong here. I think someone wanted Leo dead and they found a way to orchestrate it so that cops took him out. If that's true we could all be in serious danger."

"I will get to the bottom of this," Mark said.

"Best do it quick."

The paramedics rushed back in with the stretcher then very carefully shifted Cindy onto it. She cried out even so and it took all his restraint not to tear someone's head off for that.

"Where's Traci now?"

"In a taxi back to our house. Joseph and Geanie are there with the kids."

"You might want to go home with Joseph and Geanie until we figure this out," Jeremiah said.

He stood shakily to his feet. His ankle was sore. He must have smacked it when he hit the ground. It would take his weight, just barely. "Escort us to the ambulance, please."

"You've got it," Mark said, scrambling to his feet as well.

Mark let the paramedics take Cindy out. Jeremiah followed on the heels of the second man and Mark walked beside him. The ambulance was parked in the street and it only took a few seconds for them to load Cindy into the back of it. Jeremiah climbed in after, wincing as his ankle threatened to give way under the strain.

"I called the captain. He should be here shortly. Something this bad, I figured I needed to bring him in straight away," Mark said as he stood at the back doors of the ambulance.

"Fine," Jeremiah said. "Just, do me a favor and don't let anyone go snooping around in there. Wouldn't want them finding anything of mine."

"I'll do my best," Mark said.

Jeremiah nodded. "I'll call you once I know anything."

"Same here."

Mark closed the doors and a moment later the ambulance took off. True to his word the one paramedic administered some morphine to Cindy who was whimpering. Once he was finished Jeremiah was able to move closer and hold her hand.

"I love you."

"I love you, too," she said.

The ambulance hit a pothole and she cried out in pain. Jeremiah clenched his free hand into a fist. When he found whoever was responsible for this entire mess he'd make them sorry they'd ever heard of Leo or Cindy.

"Ssh, it's okay. It's going to be just fine," he said, trying to keep his voice low and soothing.

"Are we almost there?" she asked, her voice thin and thready.

"We should be getting close," he said.

"Just another minute," the paramedic sitting in the back with them said. "We'll get you fixed up in no time."

Suddenly there was a shouted oath from the driver and the ambulance careened wildly. Then Jeremiah heard the unmistakable sound of a high-powered rifle firing a single bullet.

12

Someone is coming to finish the job, Jeremiah realized. What was worse was that he was unarmed. His mind began racing. He thought about the sound of the shot, trying to determine what direction it had come from. He noted the swerving of the ambulance. Given that the driver had shouted before the ambulance started to go out of control he had likely seen someone or something in the road ahead of him. They were still moving, spinning back slightly.

"I'm going out that door. You close it after me," Jeremiah yelled at the paramedic in the back with him.

The man was terrified. He'd clearly heard the gunshot, too. He didn't say anything just moved closer while still bracing himself against the wall. Jeremiah prayed that he was right about the location of the shooter in relation to the ambulance and then he hit the door and threw himself out, tucking and rolling as he landed. He came up on his feet. His ankle hurt like the devil but held his weight as he tried to spot the shooter.

After a second he concluded that he was right and the ambulance was still between him and whoever was trying to kill them. They were on the back road into the hospital, the one only ambulances took so there were no cars or pedestrians around.

Nice and isolated.

There were trees lining both sides of the road. As the ambulance came to a stop Jeremiah took a chance and dashed ten feet to conceal himself behind them. He waited, heart pounding, searching for movement. His ankle was throbbing even more. The sprain hadn't been bad, but every second that he pushed it he was just making it worse. It was only a matter of time before it gave out on him so he had to make every movement count.

Finally, he saw a figure dressed in dark clothes carrying a rifle. He walked down the side of the ambulance and approached the closed doors in the back.

"Open up!" the man shouted.

Jeremiah gritted his teeth. The man was ten feet away. Timing was going to be everything. He wasn't square with the back of the ambulance but instead stood at an angle. If Jeremiah moved from his hiding place the man would see him for sure.

He could move up the tree line until he could cross in front of the ambulance, come down the side and sneak up behind him, but that would take too long. He could rush him and hope that the man would be surprised enough that he wouldn't be able to get his rifle up in time to get off a clean shot, but the odds weren't great on that one. There weren't any rocks nearby that he could throw to create a distraction.

The paramedic shouted something, but Jeremiah couldn't make out what it was. The gunman turned slightly, facing the back of the ambulance more directly. Just a hair more and Jeremiah could be on him before the man saw him.

Suddenly Jeremiah saw the doors of the ambulance move slightly. The paramedic was going to open it. Jeremiah tensed as the gunman raised his rifle.

It was now or never. Jeremiah leaped out from behind the tree. The gunman jerked his head toward him just as the ambulance door opened and the paramedic discharged a fire extinguisher directly into the man's face.

The gunman staggered backward and Jeremiah tackled him around the knees. The man went down like a lead weight, smacking his head hard on the asphalt. Jeremiah ripped the rifle from his hands and stepped back, training the weapon on the assailant.

The man didn't move. He'd hit his head hard enough to knock him unconscious, but Jeremiah wasn't taking any chances. He thought about shooting him for good measure, but they'd never get answers from a dead man.

"I got him!" Jeremiah called out.

The ambulance door flew open the rest of the way. The paramedic was standing there, holding the fire extinguisher.

"Smart thinking," Jeremiah told him.

"Is he dead?"

"You tell me. I'll keep him covered until we know."

The paramedic jumped down. He circled the body warily. He got up above the man's head, well out of arm's reach, then finally reached down and took the man's pulse.

"He's alive, but he's out," he announced after a few seconds.

Just then the driver of the ambulance came around back. He was ashen. "Who is that guy?"

"That's what I intend to find out. You have any restraints?"

The man nodded. "We've got the ability to immobilize him."

"Do it."

The two men scrambled to get the gunman onto a gurney and then strapped him down tightly. Once they were done Jeremiah pulled out his phone and called Mark.

"Hey, are the doctors checking out Cindy?" the detective asked.

"We haven't made it to the hospital yet. We were ambushed. Gunman waylaid us. We're okay and we've got him subdued in the back of the ambulance."

There was silence on the other end.

"Mark, you still there?"

"What is happening?" Mark asked, his voice barely a whisper.

"I don't know, but we need to find out fast. You need to send a couple of men you trust to take charge of this guy."

"I'm sending myself."

"No, I want you at the house until the other police clear out of there."

"Okay, then I'll call Liam."

"Isn't he still on bedrest?"

"To hell with bedrest. He can come supervise at least."

"Okay, thanks," Jeremiah said, feeling better. "We're on the back road to the emergency room, the one the ambulances use. And make sure to tell people not to shoot the guy holding the rifle, because that's me."

"Got it. I'll have him there in ten minutes."

Jeremiah hung up and took a deep breath. He went to the back of the ambulance.

"Cindy? How are you doing, darling?"

"Hurts," she panted. "And I think I'm going to throw up."

"I can give her something for that," the one paramedic said. "Could be the pain or a reaction to the morphine."

"Or the car skidding all over the road," Jeremiah noted. The paramedic nodded.

"Hold tight, sweetheart, we're going to get you into the ER just as soon as we can," Jeremiah called out to Cindy.

Unfortunately, this was an active crime scene and since her injuries weren't life threatening he didn't think it a good idea to send the ambulance on until Liam had arrived and had a chance to at least look the scene over.

While they waited his mind was racing, trying to piece everything together. Despite the timing of it all he didn't think that either the attack that killed Leo or this one was orchestrated by terrorists who had it out for him. That didn't feel right. He truly believed Leo had been the target the first time around. That left the question of this second attack.

Maybe whoever had planned the whole thing had used this as a backup in case Leo was only injured and not killed at Cindy's. Or, perhaps, someone also had it in for Cindy and had missed their chance back at the house for some reason.

There was no doubt in his mind that the unconscious man strapped to the gurney had killed people before. However, he lacked the catlike reflexes and skill to have been the one who placed the knife on Jeremiah's table without him noticing.

"So many people want us dead," he muttered to himself.

It was an unpleasant thought. He'd worked very hard to disappear, to remove himself forever from his old life. Yet here it was, surrounding them and endangering the woman he loved.

Jeremiah's dark thoughts were finally interrupted by the distant sound of a siren. He hoped it was Liam on his way and not some of the other police. Two minutes later Liam's car slid to a stop ten feet away. The detective opened the door and gingerly stepped out of the car. His arm was in a cast and he moved stiffly. The broken ribs were still clearly hurting him. He marched straight up to Jeremiah.

"Rabbi, can you please tell me what's going on? Mark called and told me to get out here, but he wasn't making any sense."

"A SWAT team invaded Cindy's house, killing a friend of hers. I had to knock her to the ground so she wouldn't get shot and it looks like her arm is broken. The ambulance was taking us to the ER when a gunman attacked us. The paramedic and I subdued him. He's now in the ambulance unconscious and restrained."

Liam stared slack-jawed at Jeremiah.

"What's wrong?" Jeremiah asked.

"I owe Mark an apology. I thought he'd gone off his rocker, but apparently not."

"Trust me, I wish this was all just a nightmare," Jeremiah said.

"I bet. Okay, a team is on their way to inspect the scene and take the shooter into custody."

"Whatever we can do to get Cindy into the ER fast, let's do it," Jeremiah said. "I also need to get off my ankle."

"What's wrong with it?"

"Sprained it back at the house. Been making it worse ever since. I can feel it swelling."

"Got it. Just give me a minute."

Other officers showed up five minutes later. The man was still unconscious so a decision was made to take both Cindy and him to the ER. There was no more room in the back of the ambulance so Jeremiah convinced the driver to let him ride up front with him. They were less than a mile from their destination, but he didn't want to take any chances.

The ER appeared to be crowded but showing up in an ambulance with a police escort gave them instant access. In a matter of moments Jeremiah was in a room with Cindy and officers were off in another room with the man who had tried to kill them.

The paramedics had given her enough medication that she was pretty out of it which was a good thing. Fortunately the wait was surprisingly short before an orderly showed up to take Cindy for x-rays. Jeremiah insisted on going with them and then waited outside the room. When she was done they retreated back to the room in the ER.

Jeremiah asked the orderly for some ice and when the man brought it back he propped his leg up on the second chair in the room and began to ice his ankle. Time seemed to crawl by then.

Finally, the doctor came in with the x-rays. He glanced at Jeremiah. "You okay?"

"Just a sprain, I'll be fine," Jeremiah said.

"Did that happen here?"

"No, before I got here."

"Okay." The doctor turned toward Cindy. "Well, young lady, it looks like you fractured your arm in two places, just below the elbow."

Jeremiah winced. He'd been afraid of that.

"Does that mean I'm going to be in a cast?" Cindy asked, slurring her words slightly.

"Unfortunately, the fractures are too close to the elbow and we can't immobilize the elbow for more than ten days without permanently losing function in it. So, we're going to set you up with a sling to wear."

"Oh joy," Cindy groaned.

"It could be a lot worse," Jeremiah said.

In his mind he'd replayed tackling her to the ground a hundred times, trying to think if there was anything he could have done differently. So far he hadn't come up with anything, but he felt terrible that her arm was fractured. He had hurt her even though he had been trying to save her.

He shook his head. That kind of thinking wasn't going to help.

"It will take about six weeks before you can really use the arm, but in that time make sure you move it around gently so as to keep from losing range of motion. You'll want to sleep with the sling on for the first couple of weeks to avoid injuring the arm. I'll give you a prescription for some painkillers you can take for the first few days; then you can switch to whichever over-the-counter medicine works best for you."

"Okay," Cindy said.

"A nurse will come in shortly and set you up with everything and then we can get you out of here," he said.

The doctor left and Cindy groaned.

"You okay?" Jeremiah asked.

"There goes my self-defense training," Cindy said with a sigh.

"Not necessarily. There are many things I can teach you that only require one hand or even no hands." Frankly he was relieved that was what was uppermost on her mind at the moment.

"Yeah?"

"Absolutely," he said with a smile. "We'll get started tomorrow if you're not in too much pain."

"Promise?"

"I promise."

She was silent for a moment and then a sob escaped her. "I can't believe they killed him."

Jeremiah reached out and gripped her left hand. "I know," he said.

"They broke down my door, invaded my house, and killed my friend. How does that happen?"

"I don't know, but we'll find out," he said.

Tears were rolling down her cheeks. "He didn't do anything."

"I know," he said, heart breaking for her.

"I don't understand."

And he knew that hurt and terrified her more than anything. He'd learned one thing about Cindy. She could handle a tremendous amount if it at least made sense, if she understood the motivations behind the violence. Random acts were what sent her into a tailspin. Until she understood what had happened she wouldn't be able to rest.

He took a deep breath. After this, making the house feel comfortable and safe to her was going to take more than changing a few pictures on the walls. At the very least they would need to reconfigure the living room and change out the furniture before she could stop seeing the tragedy play out over and over every time she tried to be in that space.

A figure stepped into the room. Jeremiah looked up, expecting a nurse, and was surprised to see Mark instead. "Everyone's left the house," he said before Jeremiah could ask.

Jeremiah nodded and Mark sat down in the chair on the other side of Cindy. "How are you doing?" he asked softly.

"Terrible," she said.

"Her arm is fractured just below the elbow. They can't cast it, so she's going to be in a sling."

"I'm sorry. I'm so very, very sorry," Mark said.

"Has anyone been able to tell you what happened?" Jeremiah asked.

"Apparently a 911 call came in that a gunman had taken hostages at the house."

"What? That's ridiculous. Nothing could have been farther from the truth. Where did the call originate from?"

"I'm looking into that. We also have one SWAT member unaccounted for."

"What does that mean?"

"It means by the time it was all over there was one less guy than there was at the start."

A chill danced up Jeremiah's spine. "Do they know who?"

"No. A couple of the guys showed up in full gear ready to go. Noone saw the face of the extra man."

"So, this could have been an orchestrated hit."

"Heck of a way to do it," Mark muttered.

"And the guy who attacked the ambulance? Is he awake and talking yet?"

"Not yet. But as soon as he does wake up I'll make sure he feels the need to say something," Mark muttered darkly.

"So, nothing on him?"

Mark cleared his throat. "Not entirely. They found a car parked not that far away. In the trunk there was SWAT gear."

"So, he was the missing man?"

Mark nodded. "Frankly, it's a relief in some ways. Pine Springs doesn't need any more crooked cops."

"Especially since the good cops are hard enough to keep in line as it is," Jeremiah said.

"Is that directed at me?" Mark asked.

"Take it as you will."

"Thanks."

"So, are they releasing Cindy soon?" Mark asked.

"As soon as the nurse sets us up with the sling and prescription."

"I've called Joseph and Geanie and let them know to expect you tonight."

"I can take Cindy to my place," Jeremiah said.

"No, you really can't," Mark said.

Something in his tone struck Jeremiah as odd. "Why not?"

Mark cleared his throat. "Because, we don't know for sure who the gunman was really after. Either one of you could be his intended target."

"But he's here in the hospital," Cindy spoke up, sounding tired.

Mark refused to look at her, instead locking eyes with Jeremiah. "Whatever's going down, he had help. The 911 caller was a woman. If you make the mistake of trying to go to either of your houses right now, there's a very real chance it will kill you."

13

"But my parents are showing up Saturday," Cindy blurted out.

"Now might not be the best time," Mark said.

"What if they insist on coming?"

"Then it's a good thing Joseph and Geanie have a ton of guestrooms."

For just a fleeting moment she thought she saw a look of relief on Jeremiah's face. She knew that thanks to the pain and the medication and the shock of everything that she wasn't thinking clearly. She couldn't see, though, how this could be anything less than a total and complete disaster. She stared at both men but neither of them seemed to have anything else to say.

The curtains moved and a nurse presented herself. "Alright, honey, let's get you fixed up so you can go home," the woman said cheerily.

"But I'm not going home," Cindy said.

"Well, wherever," the woman said, faltering only slightly.

Part of her brain was telling her it was for the best. After what had happened that night she wasn't sure she wanted to go back. Ever. A sickening thought occurred to her and she looked sharply at Mark.

"Who cleans up the blood?" she asked.

Mark took a deep breath. "There are services that handle that. Don't worry. The department will take care of it and the place will be better than new when this is all over."

She wished there was someone she could hire to scrub her brain of all the terrible images that kept replaying over and over in her head. The nurse was talking again, saying something about the sling. Cindy realized she should pay attention because she certainly didn't want to be in the hospital any longer than she had to be.

"Here, we'll give you a little space for a minute," Mark said, clamping his hand down on Jeremiah's shoulder.

~

Mark had to practically drag Jeremiah out into the hall with him. He knew the rabbi was afraid to leave Cindy alone. He didn't blame him so he positioned them where Jeremiah could watch Cindy's cubicle.

"You're sure no one found any of my things at Cindy's house?" Jeremiah asked, jaw clenched.

"Positive. What all have you got stashed there anyway?"

Jeremiah glanced at him and there was enough darkness in his gaze to force Mark to take a step backward.

"You know what? It's probably better I don't know. I mean, Joseph's rich and he stashes money. You're…you…and you stash weapons. I get it. Honestly, I do."

"With Leo dead someone's probably hoping the police will go ahead and pin that murder on him," Jeremiah said.

"At least one," Mark said with a sigh.

"What do you mean?" Jeremiah asked sharply.

"Just a hunch. I have a feeling someone wants dead Leo to take the fall for Rose's murder, too."

Jeremiah scowled. "Is that even possible?"

Mark passed a hand through his hair. "I don't know. Maybe. Even we've been complaining that two killers attending the same bachelor party is one too many. With Leo dead Cartwright and his attorney could make an argument that he was being threatened or blackmailed by Leo, framed by him even."

"Except for the part where Cartwright shot that one guy in front of Cindy and would have shot her if you hadn't showed up."

"He could still try to claim some sort of duress."

"Especially if the witnesses are dead," Jeremiah growled.

"You think the assassin was supposed to take out Cindy, too?"

"Why else would he have hit the ambulance? If it was about me, he could have shot and killed me easily. I was on top of her, though, and it would have been harder to get a fatal shot in, especially without tipping his hand right then and there."

Mark swore and yanked out his phone. He called Liam.

"It's not over yet?" his partner asked, tired sounding.

"We've got to get eyes on Beau."

"Rose's coworker?"

"Yes. Whoever took out Leo might be trying to clean up Cartwright's mess, including killing those who can testify against him. He shot Beau the night we caught him."

"I'll get some uniforms right on it."

"Can you go with them? You don't have to stay. Just make sure he's okay."

"Consider it done," Liam said before hanging up.

Mark pocketed his phone and turned to look at Jeremiah who was staring at him through narrowed lids.

"What?"

"Looks like we won't be the only ones heading to Joseph and Geanie's."

"I'm not sending Beau there."

"Not Beau. You. You were the third witness that night."

Mark swore under his breath. He closed his eyes for a moment then with a resigned sigh pulled his phone back out and called Traci. She answered on the first ring. Clearly she'd been waiting for information.

"Are they okay?"

"They're fine. Cindy's got a broken arm, but is otherwise okay. You better pack us a suitcase, though. We're all going to Joseph and Geanie's."

"Why?"

"I'll explain when I get there. That should be in about an hour."

"Okay. Love you."

"Love you, too."

He hung up. "This day just keeps getting better and better. We need to figure this out and fast."

"Cartwright's ex-fianceé showed up at the church and harassed Cindy," Jeremiah said.

"What?"

"Yeah. She blames Cindy for ruining the wedding."

"Is the woman mental?" Mark asked.

"She must be. She hit Cindy."

Mark was shocked. A terrible suspicion flooded through his brain. "You didn't...pay her a visit afterward did you?"

"No, but I will if she's behind what happened tonight," Jeremiah said.

"Yeah, let's try to avoid that," Mark said fervently.

"Apparently she's convinced that Cartwright is innocent."

"Then she is insane. Great. More fun. I think I should go have a little chat with her."

"After you get Traci and the twins safely moved."

"Of course."

"And after you get body armor on."

"I'll pick a vest up at the precinct."

"Then we'll go together."

"And that's a big 'no'. You're not a cop. I can't take you with me."

"Do you care to try and stop me?" Jeremiah asked, his voice growing very soft.

The hair stood up on the back of Mark's neck. When Jeremiah got quiet like that it scared him. The man was dangerous at the best of times. With a little provocation, though...

Mark didn't want to think about it.

"Hopefully our killer will wake up soon and we can find out who put him up to this and what their plans are," Mark hastened to say.

The nurse exited Cindy's cubicle and walked toward them. "I left the prescription and the paperwork with her. She's good to go."

~

As the mansion came into view Jeremiah felt himself relax slightly. At least he felt like Cindy would be safe there.

"Here we are at Coulter's Castle," Mark quipped. "Home to so many spontaneous gatherings of the hunted and haunted."

"That's not funny," Cindy said, her voice tired.

Mark grimaced. "Sorry."

Jeremiah got out of the car as Mark stopped in front of the entrance. He helped Cindy out. Once on her feet she stood for a moment, swaying slightly, as she stared at the mansion.

"I don't have anything with me," she said at last.

"That's okay, whatever Joseph and Geanie don't have I'm sure they can buy you," Mark said. "And if we're all very lucky this will be over in the morning."

"And if we're not very lucky?" Cindy asked.

"Then we're all stuck here hanging out with each other for a while," Mark said.

Jeremiah knew that Mark was trying to make light of the whole situation. Given how shell-shocked Cindy looked he didn't blame him.

The front door opened and Geanie came bounding out, her face scrunched up in concern. She had a baby on her hip.

"Wait, is that my daughter?" Mark asked in surprise.

"Looks as though," Jeremiah said.

Geanie did her best to hug Cindy with the baby in her arms. Then she glanced into the car. "Mark Walters you turn off that engine right now," she said sternly. "You're not going anywhere."

"Um, excuse me?" Mark asked.

"We were still at your house when you called. Everyone's here now. Traci and Ryan are inside with Joseph. Come on inside."

"Yes, ma'am," Mark said, turning off the engine as she had ordered.

"You'll get a call when our guy wakes up, right?" Jeremiah asked.

"I've told every officer guarding him and every hospital staff member to call me the moment he stirs," Mark said.

"Good. I think some rest is in order then for all of us."

"If you say so," Mark said, locking eyes with Jeremiah. "I do."

Mark nodded and got out of the car. "I hope Traci packed my pajamas," he muttered.

"If not, I'm sure you can borrow some, too," Jeremiah said.

Mark sighed.

Geanie began herding them all toward the house. She had a smile fixed on her face, but Jeremiah could tell she was worried. She should be. They all should. What happened at Cindy's place had been a nightmare and until they figured out who was behind it they all needed to sleep with one eye open. Even if they were at Coulter Castle.

The brazenness with which the killer had joined the SWAT team was stunning. Jeremiah couldn't help but anticipate what was going to happen when the man was awake and they were able to question him. It was likely that he wouldn't break easily. That was okay. Jeremiah might be a bit rusty but he hadn't forgotten how to make people talk.

"I don't like it," Mark said with a scowl as the two of them trailed the others inside.

"What?"

"Whatever it is you're thinking of doing. It makes me nervous."

"It should," Jeremiah said.

"That doesn't make me feel better."

"I'm not trying to make you feel better."

"I wish you would. Just once," Mark said with a sigh.

"Really?" Jeremiah asked.

Mark sighed again. "No, but I wish you'd let me in on what you're thinking."

"That wouldn't be a good idea."

"And why not?"

"You're already nervous enough."

"Some days it's hard being your friend. You know that?"

"Some days it's a good thing you are," Jeremiah growled.

"Trust me, you don't think I know the kind of problems you and I would have if we weren't friends?"

"Don't get in the way when I…question…that guy tomorrow."

"That's going to be a touch hard. First off, there are police swarming all over his room."

"So, do yourself and them a favor and distract them for me."

"Second," Mark continued, ignoring what Jeremiah had just said, "I can't be involved in anything that looks even remotely like what I did to that guy a couple of years ago."

Jeremiah turned to him. "Mark, you told me how you tortured that guy, what you did to him."

"Your point being?" Mark asked gruffly.

Jeremiah stopped just before they reached the door into the house. "Trust me when I say that what I'm going to do to this guy won't look even remotely the same."

Jeremiah stared intently at Mark as the man's face went pale and his pupils dilated. Then he turned and walked into the house before the detective could respond.

Cindy and the others were in the kitchen where Joseph was serving up some hot dogs and potato salad. Jeremiah's stomach growled. He hadn't had a chance to finish dinner earlier. He was glad to see Cindy take a hot dog and bite into it. She would need the protein to keep her strength up. Sometimes when people had received a terrible shock they didn't eat as much as they should for a while afterward.

Jeremiah sat down on one of the stools lining the counter.

"Can I offer you a hot dog?" Joseph asked as he handed a paper plate to Jeremiah.

"You can offer me two, and I'll eat them both."

Joseph grinned and served him up the hot dogs and a hearty helping of potato salad. After a minute Mark sat down next to Jeremiah. He could feel the tension coming off the other man, but at the moment that wasn't his problem. He knew Mark would prefer if he kept him more in the dark, but that wasn't necessarily the best course of action.

Traci and Geanie disappeared for a couple of minutes, going to put the babies to bed. After a moment's hesitation Cindy followed them.

Joseph grabbed himself a hot dog and sat down to eat with Jeremiah and Mark.

"Geanie is really good with them," Mark commented.

"Yeah," Joseph said, smiling faintly. "She would make a great mom."

There was something slightly wistful in the way that he said it. Jeremiah knew that the couple were trying to get pregnant, but he didn't say anything.

"So, together again," Joseph said a moment later, his customary grin returning in full force. "You know, these sleepovers are becoming a habit."

A sudden bit of black fluff jumped onto the counter. Wide yellow eyes stared at Jeremiah.

"Blackie?" he asked.

"Yeah, we swung by and picked him up. Don't worry, we have Captain, too. Right now he's in the other room snoozing with Clarice and Buster."

"Thank you," Jeremiah said. "How?"

"We had copies of your keys made a while back," Joseph said before biting into his hot dog.

Jeremiah shook his head and grinned. "I must be rubbing off on you."

Joseph shrugged. "It seemed like a no-brainer," he said. "It makes it easier for the fur babies to have play dates."

Jeremiah chuckled. Blackie rubbed his head against Jeremiah's hand then sniffed at the hot dog Jeremiah was holding. He broke off a piece and offered it to the cat who took it after a moment and settled down to eat it.

"We found him hiding under the bed," Joseph said. "It took a minute to find him. We were starting to worry that he'd gotten out during…everything."

"How bad did the place look?" Jeremiah asked.

"Really bad."

"We'll have it cleaned before Cindy steps foot back in it," Mark said.

"I'm thinking we need to rearrange the furniture in the living room, too. Maybe even get some new furniture so that it looks different and doesn't instantly remind her of tonight," Jeremiah said.

"I'm thinking it would be easier if we just bought her a new house," Joseph said.

Jeremiah studied the other man's face. "You're not kidding, are you?"

"Nope. I saw that living room. So did Geanie. Geanie lived there for a while, you know, and yet I don't see her ever going back inside for a visit after tonight."

"If you're handing out new houses, you know ours has seen its share of trauma," Mark said, smiling impishly.

Joseph rolled his eyes. "I think I should just have a couple more houses built up here on the hill. It would make a lot of things easier."

Jeremiah chuckled. "And a lot of things stranger."

"I would say that they couldn't get any stranger," Joseph said, "but I'm pretty sure they'd find a way to."

"Please, we don't need stranger in any of our lives," Mark said.

Mark's phone rang and the detective jumped. He dug the phone out of his pocket. "Hello? Yes, this is Detective Walters. What? Say that again. How? Okay."

Mark hung up. All color had drained from his face and he looked like he was going to be sick.

Jeremiah felt his stomach clench. "What happened?"

"That was the hospital. Our killer was just murdered."

14

Mark was stunned. There were police right outside the man's room. At least, there should have been.

"How?" Jeremiah asked.

"I don't know," Mark said, passing his hand over his face.

"Someone's cleaning up their loose ends."

"They must have been afraid that he'd talk," Mark said.

"Are you okay? You look like you're going to be sick," Joseph said.

Mark pulled at his collar. "I think I need some air."

His phone rang again and he answered it as a feeling of dread settled in the pit of his stomach.

"Hello?"

"Hey, it's Liam," his partner said, voice grim. "We've got a problem."

"Yeah, the hospital just called me."

"What?"

"The killer was murdered in the hospital."

There was a pause and then Liam said, "That's not the problem I'm talking about."

"Oh hell, what's happened?" Mark asked starting to feel sick to his stomach. He could hear noise in the other room. Traci's laugh rang out distinctively in sharp contrast to how he was feeling.

"Beau is dead. Looks like he was killed earlier this evening."

Mark looked up at Jeremiah. "Beau is dead."

"What?" he heard a woman gasp. He spun around on his stool and saw Cindy, standing in the doorway, her skin ashen. Several steps behind her Geanie and Traci froze.

"Mark, we have got to get a handle on this," Liam said.

"Yeah," he muttered.

His head was spinning and the knife wound was throbbing. He tried to remember how long it had been since he'd taken some pain killers. He began to tilt sideways on the chair. Suddenly Jeremiah's hand clamped down on his shoulder. Mark closed his eyes, fighting the waves of pain and nausea that were rolling over him.

"Liam, when you're done there, come on up to Joseph and Geanie's house so we can get this sorted," he said.

"Are you okay?" Liam asked sharply.

"No, no, I'm not."

He was hot and cold all at the same time. The wooziness got worse and he felt like the room was tilting.

"Mark!" he heard Jeremiah call from what seemed far away.

Then he was falling.

~

Cindy watched Mark start to slide off his chair. She tried to shout a warning, but no sound came out. Jeremiah grabbed Mark as he was falling and was able to gently lower him to the ground. Traci screamed and rushed past Cindy to drop next to Mark.

He's dead, the thought flashed through her mind. *Just like Leo. Just like Beau.* She opened her mouth to say something, to ask if he was alive, but no sound came out.

She began to shake uncontrollably and it felt like the temperature had just dropped twenty degrees in the room.

She could hear Jeremiah saying something, but she couldn't comprehend the words. The others began talking as well, but they might as well have been speaking gibberish. Then she saw Mark's fingers twitch. He was alive. She tried to hold that in her mind, fixate on that and not on those who were dead or how cold she was. Pain was shooting through her body in unconnected places at seemingly random intervals.

Traci had pulled open Mark's shirt and Jeremiah was looking at some bandages. Joseph was on his phone calling someone. Geanie moved up next to Cindy and put her hand on her arm. Cindy could see Geanie's hand, but she couldn't feel it.

"What on earth is happening?" Geanie asked, bewildered sounding.

Cindy wanted to tell her that she didn't know. That, in fact, she didn't know anything anymore. But all she could do was stare. Geanie moved around to stand in front of her. Cindy looked at her and all she could do was just blink.

"We need to get you somewhere quiet," Geanie said.

Geanie put her arm around her and pulled Cindy in the direction of the living room. At first it was as though Cindy's feet didn't want to move, but finally the left one did, followed by the right. Geanie kept her going, propelling her along with steady pressure until they made it in the other room.

"We're going to get you down on the couch so you can be more comfortable," Geanie said.

Cindy could only nod to indicate that she understood. When they made it to the couch Geanie had to physically push her down onto it. Cindy landed on the soft cushions and felt some of the stiff muscles along her spine go slack as they no longer had to keep her upright. She closed her eyes, but the world was still there, pressing in against her eyelids, demanding her attention no matter how much she didn't want to give it.

"It's going to be okay," Geanie said. "Let me go get you a glass of ice water."

Cindy was already too cold. She shook her head slightly.

"Hot tea?"

Cindy nodded.

"I'll be right back."

Cindy sat, struggling to process everything she was feeling. She finally gave up because it was too much. Instead she just concentrated on breathing slowly and evenly.

When Geanie returned with the tea Cindy forced her eyes open and took the mug from her. It was a huge mug with The Zone logo on it. It was heavy enough that it was awkward to hold in her left hand. Cindy took a sip of the steaming liquid. It was nearly too hot, but somehow it made her feel better. She needed the heat to chase away the cold that was numbing her. She took another sip and then stared at the mug.

"What's wrong?" Geanie asked worriedly.

"You don't have teacups?" Cindy asked, finally finding her voice.

Geanie stared at her for a moment and then burst out laughing so hard she fell down in the chair next to the couch.

"Here I am worried that you're having some kind of psychotic break and you're asking me why I didn't put the tea in a teacup," Geanie said, continuing to howl with laughter.

"You have the world's biggest kitchen with every gadget there is," Cindy said. "I guess for Christmas I have to get you teacups, though."

Geanie's laughter was helping to warm her insides just as much as the tea was. If she was laughing that hard then things couldn't be as bleak as Cindy was imagining.

Geanie wiped the tears from her eyes. "We have plenty of tea sets, including one that's older than this country. I just thought you needed a big, hot mug and not a tiny little sipper cup. Next time I'll know better and get out the bone china."

"What's going on out there?" Cindy asked before taking another sip of the tea.

"Joseph's called our doctor to come out and take a look at Mark's injury. Jeremiah's worried it's getting infected."

"Why not take him to the hospital?"

Geanie winced. "He refuses to hear of it. He doesn't want to have to explain to anyone how he got the injury."

"I didn't know doctors still made house calls."

Geanie shrugged. "Ours does. Then again, he only has a handful of patients."

"Ah."

"So, are you okay?" Geanie asked, leaning forward.

"I'm better at the moment," Cindy said. "I'm wanting this day to end in the worst way."

"Then why don't you go to bed and get some sleep? I know you could use it."

"I'm afraid to be alone with my thoughts," she admitted. "I don't want to try to go to sleep and just see…everything all over again. You know?"

"I understand," Geanie said, biting her lip. She hesitated a moment then continued. "I'll have the doctor look you over as well. I think you went into shock."

"I'm very, very cold."

"Yeah, I think that's shock."

"I'll be okay."

"I know, but it doesn't hurt to have him spend five minutes."

"Okay, but after he's looked over Mark."

"Of course."

As if on cue Jeremiah walked through the door supporting Mark. They moved over to one of the couches and Jeremiah helped the detective down.

"I'm fine, stop fussing," Mark said irritably.

"You keep being difficult and next time I'll carry you," Jeremiah warned.

"Wouldn't that be a sight? No, thank you. I don't care to have you carry me across the threshold like some blushing bride."

"Actually, I was thinking over my shoulder like a sack of potatoes."

"You do that and I'll shoot you," Mark threatened.

Jeremiah snorted derisively. "I've been shot before, and by better marksmen than you."

"I think my honor has just been questioned."

"No, but your aim has been," Jeremiah countered with a roll of his eyes. He turned toward Geanie. "I hope our other patient is more tractable."

"I'm not a patient," Cindy said.

Geanie shrugged.

"Switch?" Jeremiah asked Geanie.

"It's worth a try," she said, getting up and moving closer to Mark.

Jeremiah came over and sat down next to Cindy on the couch. He put an arm around her and she gladly leaned her head against his shoulder. "How are you?" he asked gently.

She felt like she would burst into tears at any moment, but she fought the sensation. She didn't want to sob or scream or grieve. She just wanted to sit quietly and enjoy the feel of his shirt against her cheek and listen to the soothing sound of his voice.

"I've been worse."

It was true. Not often, but she had been worse.

He rubbed her shoulder slowly and she scooted as close as she could to him.

"It's going to be okay," he said softly.

She closed her eyes. He kept talking soft and low, just for her. It was soothing and the exhaustion that had been hovering at the edges of her consciousness finally overtook her.

~

It had been a bad day. Jeremiah was grateful when Cindy finally nodded off. She was going to need a while to recover both physically and mentally from what had happened at her house. He was worried she wouldn't be able to. Getting new furniture and rearranging the living room was a top priority. He needed to make sure that happened before she returned home in order to minimize the trauma and the flashbacks she'd have when she stepped foot in the door. Of course, that was going to be tricky without being able to go back to the house yet. He'd just have to make sure she stayed at Joseph and Geanie's a day or two longer than he did.

He pushed a strand of hair out of her eyes and she didn't stir. He glanced over at Geanie and Mark. Geanie was talking softly to Mark whose eyes were looking a little glassy.

Suddenly Joseph entered the room followed by a tall man in his forties carrying an old fashioned doctor's bag. He took the room in at a glance then made a beeline for Mark. Geanie moved quickly out of the way.

"I'm fine," Mark said slowly.

"I'll be the judge of that," the doctor said in clipped tones. "Take off your shirt."

"I don't know you," Mark said.

He was being irrational which worried Jeremiah more.

"Dr. Baird, now you know me. Take it off or I'll remove it for you."

Jeremiah suppressed a smile. Dr. Baird didn't play around. Then again, he was probably used to dealing with some fairly stubborn, arrogant patients.

"Could I get some privacy?" Mark asked, glaring at everyone.

"No," Jeremiah said.

"Sure," Geanie said a breath later. She looked at Jeremiah. "I'm leaving you in charge."

He nodded. Geanie left the room and he refocused his attention on Mark and Dr. Baird.

"Hold still or I'll report the knife wound," Dr. Baird threatened.

"I'm a cop," Mark growled.

"I don't care if you're Batman, you need to cooperate."

"Mark, settle down," Jeremiah said.

"Is he always this combative?" Dr. Baird asked.

"Not usually this bad," Jeremiah said. "I'm worried."

"You're right to be," Dr. Baird said. "He's got a fever."

"I thought so."

"Stop talking about me!" Mark hissed. "I'm going to get up and walk out."

"And, you're done," Dr. Baird said, reaching into his bag for something.

Jeremiah saw the doctor pull out a syringe.

"I am?" Mark asked.

"Yes," Dr. Baird said, swiftly injecting Mark in the arm. "Just not in the way you think."

Seconds later Mark slumped on the couch.

"You gave him a sedative?" Jeremiah asked.

"Seemed like the safest thing for all concerned."

"Good choice."

Jeremiah watched as the doctor swiftly got Mark's shirt off and began removing the bandages. He could just make out the wound which looked ugly and red. He could hear the doctor muttering to himself as he examined it. He then cleaned out the wound and put a fresh dressing on it. He finally stripped off his gloves, dumping them in a trash bag he'd been using and stood up.

"Well?" Jeremiah asked.

"It looks worse than it is, but he definitely needs an antibiotic. I'll write a prescription. There's a twenty-four hour pharmacy near the hospital. His wife should be able to get it filled tonight. I don't want to waste time."

"Understood."

Dr. Baird turned his attention to Cindy. "Is she my other patient?"

"Yeah. She's had a terrible day. Her arm is broken. She already had it looked at in the hospital. When Mark passed out she went into shock."

"At least it looks like she's resting now. I'm not sure I want to wake her if she's been through a lot of trauma. Sleep is the best thing for her. Still, I'll listen to her heart and lungs, just to make sure everything sounds good there."

Jeremiah nodded. The doctor grabbed a stethoscope out of his bag and came over. He crouched down in front of them and listened for several seconds first to Cindy's heart then to her breathing. He nodded and put the instrument away.

"Everything sounds okay. Honestly, I can come back in the morning, but if she can sleep let's let her."

"Sounds good," Jeremiah said. "Mark's wife, Traci, should be in the other room."

"Good, I'll give her the prescription for the antibiotic."

He put his card on the coffee table. "Joseph has my number, but I'm leaving it here, just in case."

"Thank you for your help," Jeremiah said.

"Not a problem. It's what I do."

Dr. Baird left the room after gathering his stuff together. Jeremiah could hear him talking to others in the kitchen. Joseph was lucky to have a doctor that could show up when needed.

Jeremiah looked down at Cindy who was fast asleep. He settled himself down, realizing it might be several hours before she woke. That was okay. He wasn't in the mood to sleep. He had way too much on his mind.

A sudden commotion from the other room caught his attention. He could hear arguing, but couldn't make out the words. A minute later a familiar figure entered the room.

Liam stared at him, desperation in his eyes. "Jeremiah, you have to help me!"

15

Jeremiah stared at Liam intently. "What's wrong?" he asked.

"Geanie is insisting on going into work tomorrow and taking Cindy if she wants to go," the detective said.

Jeremiah narrowed his eyes. "I'm not sure that's the smartest idea."

"That's what I'm saying."

"I'll have a talk with both of them," Jeremiah said.

"Thank you. The last thing we need is any more uncertainty, more unpredictability, more-"

"Casualties?" Jeremiah finished.

"Exactly." Liam glanced over at Mark and it was easy to read the concern on his face. "How is he?"

"He'll be okay. The doctor cleaned things up and prescribed an antibiotic."

"That's a relief."

Liam sat down heavily in a chair. He had a cast on his left arm and he looked ragged.

"I thought you were supposed to be on medical leave," Jeremiah said.

"Wouldn't that be nice," Liam said wearily.

"So, what happened to Beau?"

"It looked like a mugging gone wrong, but I think we all know better," Liam said.

"In light of everything else that's happened, I'd say so."

"Dude didn't deserve that."

"Most don't," Jeremiah said quietly.

"This whole thing is just a mess. I've never seen a case go so sideways after the killer is in custody."

"Clearly someone wishes the man to go free. By killing or discrediting any possible witness it could just happen."

"And the only two remaining ones are in this room," Liam said.

"It didn't escape my attention. It's been a busy day."

"Is Cindy okay?" Liam asked.

"Her arm is broken. Because of where it is they can't put a cast on it."

"Rough. I can sympathize. That's going to be hard on her. I've already slammed my arm into three things. At least I was wearing a cast when I did."

"Other than that, she's in shock."

"No one can blame her for that," Liam said.

"How's Rebecca holding up after everything?" Jeremiah asked.

Liam actually flushed slightly. "She's doing okay. A lot better than I would be in her shoes."

"She's resilient, that one," Jeremiah said.

"Yeah. It's a good thing, too. It's rough being a cop's wife."

Jeremiah stared at Liam, startled. "Did I miss something?"

Liam flushed harder. "No, sorry, just… thinking ahead."

"Well, it's pretty clear where you think the relationship is going."

"The men in my family tend to know when we find the one."

"Congratulations. When do you plan on letting *her* know?" Jeremiah asked, unable to suppress a smile.

"I was thinking sooner rather than later, but I just don't know when she'll be ready to have that conversation."

Jeremiah shook his head slowly. There was a very real possibility that Liam and Rebecca would be getting married before he and Cindy did. He couldn't help but feel a twinge of jealousy. Still, Liam and Rebecca weren't them, and comparing him and Cindy to another couple was futile, especially since he was convinced there was no other couple quite like them.

~

Wednesday morning Jeremiah was unable to talk Cindy and Geanie out of going to work. Mark was alert enough to insist that they have a police detail. They relented, and now Cindy couldn't help but stare at the uniformed officer who had been sitting in the chair in front of her desk all morning.

Every time a church member came in they nearly jumped out of their skin to see the man sitting there. Cindy was getting tired of explaining that there was nothing wrong at the church. Since she didn't care to share why the two officers were actually on property, though, she was sure that the gossip mill would come up with exciting if implausible reasons for the police presence.

It had been an exhausting morning, but she figured it was better than sitting around in Geanie's house with everyone staring at each other and wondering what new calamity was about to befall them.

"Yoohoo, Cindy," Geanie called from her desk.

Cindy jerked and turned to look at her. "Sorry, what?"

"I was asking if we should get some pizza delivered for lunch given the circumstances."

Cindy took a deep breath. She would have liked to escape the office for a few minutes, but having the food come to them would be much easier under the circumstances.

"Sure."

She turned and looked at the officer in front of her desk. "Would you like some pizza?" she asked.

He grinned sheepishly. "Actually, I would."

"You know what, we should have a pizza party," Cindy blurted out.

Geanie stared at her. "Are you serious?"

"Life's too short not to have a spontaneous pizza party," Cindy said. "The staff has all been so busy we've missed our last couple of monthly meetings. Unless you had one while I wasn't here."

"No, we didn't. I'll order the pizzas and you let everyone know," Geanie said.

"Deal."

Cindy turned back to her computer and quickly emailed everyone. Seconds later Sylvia, the business manager, poked her head out of her office. "Sounds great."

~

Jeremiah wasn't happy that Cindy had decided to go into work. He understood that she was struggling for some normalcy in the midst of the horror. In his mind, though, that didn't justify the risk. And a couple of uniformed officers sitting in the office with her did little to relieve his anxiety.

Which is why he'd hacked her phone.

He should have done it ages ago. Sitting in his office at the synagogue he was able to listen to everything that was happening to Cindy through the microphone in her phone. He tried to think of it less as spying and more as a security system.

He was relieved when she and Geanie decided to have pizza delivered to the church. As it was he was struggling with his desire to go check on her and say hello. He realized he should probably give her some bonding time with her coworkers, though, especially since her being back to work was new. He had no desire to have to tangle with the pastor so soon after he had been forced to accept her back on staff. He sighed. Sometimes life seemed needlessly complicated.

There was a knock on his door. Fortunately, he was listening to Cindy's phone through an earbud so no one else would be able to hear what he was listening to.

"Come in."

Marie entered. She had been quieter than usual all morning. She stood just inside the door watching him contemplatively.

"Yes?" he asked, surprised that she wasn't saying anything.

"Are you okay?"

He forced a smile. "I'm fine."

She stared at him for several seconds. Then she walked all the way in and closed the door behind her.

"Cut the crap," she said.

"Excuse me?"

"I heard what happened. There's no way that you're fine."

"How did you-"

She held up her hand. "Please, don't insult me."

"Okay." He took a deep breath. "I'm worried to death."

"Of course you are. And she's got to be absolutely sick. So, why aren't you over there right now?"

"I'm trying not to invade her space."

"Are you kidding me?" Marie asked, glaring at him.

"No. I'm not exactly popular with her boss and I'm trying not to rock the boat."

Marie folded her arms over her chest and her cheeks burned red. She looked angrier than he could ever remember seeing her.

"What?" he asked.

"Last I checked, *God* was her boss, not some idiot pastor. And, as far as I know, the boss likes you just fine."

He was so surprised he didn't have a response. He just stared at her like an idiot. Finally he blurted out, "I didn't think you liked Cindy."

He didn't know why he said it. It was honestly the first thing that popped into his mind.

Marie sniffed. "I don't, but I respect the hell out of her and she deserves your respect and your protection."

"I don't know what to say."

"Of course you don't. Just get out of here and go check on her."

"Yes, ma'am," he said, rising quickly to his feet.

"Good," she said, opening the door and storming out.

Jeremiah hastily followed her. She sat down at her desk and didn't look up as he passed by her and headed out the front door. Every once in a while Marie surprised him and this was by far the biggest surprise of all.

~

Mark felt like crap and he wished that he could just sleep for the next three days. With everything that was going on that wasn't an option, though. He was furious that he hadn't been able to keep Cindy from going into work. He got that she was struggling for some normalcy given what had happened, but it was too dangerous. Even Jeremiah hadn't been able to talk sense into her.

For his part, he had three people he had to talk to before the day was through. First up was Gareth who had been thick as thieves with Ivan during the bachelor party. Mark drove to Rayburn NextGen Solutions, but was frustrated in his efforts when he found out that Gareth had flown out on a business trip the evening before and wouldn't be back for a few days. It seemed awfully convenient to him.

Fortunately his second interviewee of the day also worked at the company and Lloyd the accountant was indeed in his office. A minute later Mark was knocking on the man's door.

"Come in," a voice called.

Mark entered the office, shutting the door again behind him. "Are you Lloyd?"

"Yes, who are you?" the man said, looking up from a stack of papers.

"I'm Detective Mark Walters," he said, briefly flashing his badge. "I'd like to ask you some questions."

Lloyd frowned. "I don't know why you're here, but I can assure you that my books are all up to date."

"I'm not here about a money issue."

"Then why are you here?"

"I wanted to discuss Kenneth Cartwright's bachelor party."

Lloyd looked even more bewildered at that. "Why? I mean, I know he's been arrested for murdering his secretary. The whole company knows that. It's not like he talked about it at the party. I mean, it would have been helpful if he had. It would have stopped me from buying an expensive wedding present the next day. Never have glassware engraved. They won't let you return it if you do."

"Sound advice." Mark said drily. "I'm not here to talk about Kenneth murdering his secretary. I'm here to talk about what happened at the party."

"You mean besides Leo passing out and Gareth making a fool of himself trying to impress Ivan? Nothing really. There was a stripper who never actually, you know, stripped. She cut out before that. Frankly the most exciting thing that happened was I got the chance to count the total number of calories Kenneth's cousin consumed between the appetizers and the alcohol. It was astonishing."

"Wow, you really are a numbers guy, aren't you?" Mark said.

"Numbers never lie."

"Then I've got some numbers for you."

"Yeah?"

"Yeah," Mark said. "Six guys and one stripper are at a party. Two of them end up dead. What are the odds?"

Lloyd blinked at him. "Dead? Who's dead?"

"The stripper and Leo."

"What?" Lloyd asked, turning pale. "How? When?"

"The stripper was killed at the party. Leo was assassinated last night."

"What? That doesn't add up. The stripper left the party. And Leo…"

"When? When did the stripper leave the party?"

"I don't know, about half an hour after she got there I guess."

"Did you see her go?" Mark pressed.

"I… no, I didn't actually see her go. I went to the restroom and when I came back she wasn't there."

"And where was Leo?"

"He was already asleep in a chair. I didn't think he had that much to drink either."

Cindy was right. Leo hadn't had anything to do with April's death. If Lloyd was telling the truth then he hadn't had anything to do with it either.

"Did Kenneth kill her, too?" Lloyd asked.

"That's one theory."

"Well, who else… wait, you don't think I had anything to do with any of this?"

"That's what I'm here to find out," Mark said grimly. "Where was everyone else when you got back from the restroom?"

"I don't know."

"Try to remember."

"Leo's dead, too? Why?"

"Because the killer was trying to frame him for April's murder," Mark said.

"But that's preposterous. He was out cold before she left."

"I'd keep that information between us at the moment," Mark said.

"Why?"

"Because odds are good one of the other four guys at that party killed both of them, or at least, arranged to kill both of them."

"Reginald couldn't hurt a fly unless it was dipped in chocolate and served as a delicacy."

"What about Gareth?"

"Gareth?"

"Is he capable of hurting a fly?"

"I… I don't know," Lloyd said, horror creeping into his voice.

"What can you tell me about him, aside from the fact that he's out of town on a business trip?"

Lloyd looked at him sharply. "No, he's not."

"Someone in his department told me he was."

"Maybe that's what he told them, but all travel is arranged ahead of time and the paperwork would have already crossed my desk. He's not on any business trip."

"Interesting. What else can you tell me?" Mark asked.

"He's ambitious."

"A good salesman?"

"Mediocre at best. He won last year's sales competition by cheating," Lloyd said, a note of anger creeping into his voice.

"How?"

"He charmed a couple of his buddies into making massive orders which they then returned after the competition period was closed. Do you know what kind of paperwork that generates for me? Especially when there's no reason given for the return?"

"Sounds like a real prince of a guy."

"He'd like everyone to think so. He's more pauper than prince, though. I still don't know how he swung buying that Ferrari. I know how much he makes and it isn't that much."

"I heard he spent the night hitting on Ivan."

"Hitting on him? No, schmoozing him," Lloyd said.

"To what end?" Mark asked.

"I don't know, but there's something Gareth thought Ivan could get for him or do for him."

"Any idea what that might be?"

"Not really."

"But if you had to guess?"

"Money? Prestige? Gareth likes that a lot," Lloyd said.

"That's why he got the Ferrari?"

"Of course. The guy doesn't even like to drive."

"So the car is all about status."

"Has to be… You don't think… you don't think he could actually kill someone, do you?" Lloyd said, obviously struggling to process everything.

"Do you?" Mark asked pointedly.

Lloyd licked his lips. "I don't want to," he whispered.

"But you do."

Lloyd nodded slowly.

It could be an act, his way of throwing suspicion onto his coworker but Mark doubted it. Just like Leo this guy didn't feel like a killer to him.

He stood. The pain in his shoulder was creeping back in. He'd have to take some more pain killers soon. He still wanted to collapse but he had someone else he needed to talk to first.

"Thank you for your time," he said, extending his hand.

Lloyd stood awkwardly and shook it.

"If you think of anything else, give me a call," Mark said, pulling a business card out of his pocket and handing it to Lloyd. The other man took it with a nod. Mark forced a smile before turning to go. He wanted to pay a visit to Nita Rayburn.

He made it back to his car, downed some pain killers, and headed out of the company parking lot. He replayed the conversation with Lloyd in his head. He had said that Gareth wanted something from Ivan. If that was true, what could it be? And what would he have been willing to do to get it?

He liked Ivan for killing April, but he wasn't about to rule out Gareth either. It was possible that Gareth even killed April for Ivan, in order to get whatever it was he thought Ivan could or would give him.

Money, prestige, power. It had to be one or all of those that Gareth was looking for based on Lloyd's analysis. There was something there. He could feel it like a tugging sensation in his gut. What was Ivan offering? And who was he offering it to? If only he had someone who could get close to Ivan at a social function, like the gala he was going to Friday night.

That was crazy thinking. There was no way he could get someone into that event. Even if he could, the chances of them being able to get anything out of Ivan were next to impossible. Guys like that only opened up to people they wanted something from or to someone they wanted to manipulate.

He had worked himself into utter frustration by the time he reached Nita Rayburn's residence. He took a moment in the car to steel himself before getting out.

Nita lived in a mansion. It wasn't as impressive as Joseph's but it was still large. He walked up to the door. His finger was hovering over the doorbell when he heard gravel crunch behind him. Something cold and hard was shoved into the small of his neck.

"Don't move or I'll blow your head off."

16

Mark froze as every muscle in his body tightened. A dozen scenarios flashed through his mind. In more than half of them he ended up dead.

"Do you have any idea who you're pointing that thing at?" he growled.

"Yeah, a trespasser."

"Wrong. A cop."

"You're a cop?"

Mark could hear the hesitation in the other man's voice.

"That's right and you have exactly one second to lower that before I arrest you for battery."

The man behind him swore and the pressure on Mark's neck ceased. He spun around and disarmed the man in one swift move. Mark stood there, fury coursing through him, as he held the other man's gun.

"What are you doing with this?" he demanded.

"I'm security for Miss Rayburn," the man said, though he turned slightly pale.

"Didn't anyone tell you to never attack a stranger without figuring out a few things first, like who he is and whether he has legitimate business with your boss?" Mark demanded.

It had been a rough week so far and the urge to pistol whip the guy with his own gun was strong. He took several deep breaths trying to force his body to relax and let go of the fight or flight mode that it was in. He contented himself with removing the bullets from the man's gun before handing it back to him.

"Now, take me to your boss," Mark said.

"Sure, this way."

The idiot didn't even bother to ask to see his badge. He was too flustered. Mark would have thought about suggesting to Nita that she find herself a new bodyguard, but if she was the mastermind behind the recent murders he didn't want to give her any help.

Mark followed the man around the back of the house to a pool. Nita was there, lounging with a drink in hand. Her very manner screamed arrogance and entitlement, and he was so not in the mood to deal with her. He probably should have stayed home and sent Liam out to handle these interviews. His partner was supposed to be on leave, though, and he'd already had to work enough this week.

"Miss Rayburn, there's a cop here to see you," the man said nervously.

Nita looked up disdainfully. "He's a cop?"

"A detective, actually," Mark said.

"What do you want?"

"I want to know why you arranged a hit on Cindy and Leo last night."

"What?" she asked.

"Why did you hire a hitman to kill Cindy and Leo last night?"

She stared at him for a moment and then burst out with a laugh. "Someone killed that despicable secretary? That's the best thing I've ever heard!"

And in that moment Mark wanted her dead. Hatred ripped through him. The fact that she could be so callous about such a thing, and the fact that she'd wish such evil on

Cindy of all people, made him so angry he had to clench his hand tightly into a fist to keep from doing something he shouldn't.

"I'm sorry to say I had nothing to do with killing her. I'd love to congratulate whoever did, though."

He believed her. If she had hired the gunman she would know that Leo was dead but Cindy wasn't. However, he couldn't let her arrogance, her nastiness go. Someone needed to take her down a notch.

"Ma'am, you're going to have to come with me to the precinct to answer some questions."

"You're joking."

"No, I'm not. Now, are you going to come along peacefully?" Mark asked, moving his jacket aside so that she could see his handcuffs.

"You wouldn't dare!"

"If you're a danger to yourself or others, I'll be obligated to," he said, refusing to back down.

She stood abruptly, eyes glaring daggers at him. She turned and cast a sharp look at her bodyguard. "You, call my attorney."

"I don't-"

"Figure it out," she snapped.

She led the way imperiously to the front of the house where she climbed into the backseat of his car. She didn't even bother to ask to change clothes. Clearly she felt she was going to be out of there so quickly it wasn't worth it. Mark narrowed his eyes as he contemplated all the ways in which he'd like to make her life unpleasant.

~

Cindy and the others had congregated in the library for the impromptu pizza party. The mood kept vacillating between festive and somber which was a bit disconcerting. It reminded her in many ways of a funeral. Maybe that was appropriate given what had happened to Leo.

"Have another slice of pepperoni," Geanie urged.

Cindy wasn't as hungry as she'd normally be. Even the smell of the pizza wasn't as much of an enticement as it should have been.

"No, I'm okay."

"You need to eat. Keep up your strength."

"She's right," a deep voice said behind her.

Cindy turned and without thinking flung her good arm around Jeremiah's neck. As much as she'd wanted to prove that she could go to work she felt instantly safer knowing that he was there.

"Thank you," Geanie said. "Now listen to Jeremiah and have something more to eat."

~

Mark shouldn't have been surprised that Nita Rayburn's attorney made it to the precinct before he and Nita did. The man's suit probably cost more than Mark's entire wardrobe. Unlike his client, however, the attorney didn't bother with the disdain and the snobbery. Instead he was coldly efficient.

In the end all Mark could do was hold her in an interrogation room and let her sweat for a while. It was frustrating, but he got some comfort out of knowing that as indifferent as she appeared he had at least made her day more difficult.

Ultimately he decided to visit the one other person on his list in the hope that the day wouldn't be a total bust. If Gareth wasn't on a business trip like the one secretary had claimed, then he might actually be home.

Mark got in his car then hesitated. Going alone to interview a suspect was never a good thing, particularly when it was in the person's home. The encounter with Nita's bodyguard could easily have ended disastrously. Mark wasn't exactly playing at the top of his game either.

With a sigh he called Liam.

"How are you feeling?" Liam asked, skipping the usual salutation.

"Like I've been run over. I think the antibiotics are kicking my behind, too."

"They'll do that. So, what do you need?"

"A guy can't just call his partner to say hello without needing something?"

There was pointed silence on the other end.

"Fine," Mark said. "I could use someone to watch my back while I go interview a witness."

"No one else is available?"

"Right now you're the only one I trust. The captain's still sorting out the mess from last night."

"Understood. Text me the address and I'll meet you there."

"How about I pick you up? It's on the way and then you won't have to drive with your busted arm."

"And I won't be able to escape after the interview," Liam said with a twinge of sarcasm.

"Come on, bed rest is overrated."

~

After picking up a reluctant looking Liam, Mark made straight for Gareth's apartment. By the time they'd parked Mark had been able to fill his partner in on everything he'd done so far that day.

"If he's actually trying to avoid us and he has half a brain he won't be here," Liam said as they walked up to the door.

"Let's just hope he's cocky," Mark said as he rang the doorbell.

A few moments later the door swung open.

"Cocky," Liam said under his breath.

"Gareth?" Mark asked.

"Yes, can I help you?" the man answered.

"I'm Detective Walters and this is my partner. We have some questions for you."

"I'm sorry, Gentlemen, but I'm on my way to the airport. I have a business trip," Gareth said.

"Actually, I know for a fact that you don't," Mark said. "Lying to the police does not look good."

Gareth looked surprised but grudgingly stood back to let them in. Moments later the three of them were seated in a cramped family room.

"So, what is this about?" Gareth asked.

"We have some questions for you about a bachelor party you attended recently," Mark said.

"What about it?"

"How well did you know April Snow?"

"Who?" Gareth asked.

"The stripper who performed at the party," Mark said.

"Oh, well, I don't know her at all. And I would hardly say she performed at the party. She didn't stick around long enough to dance. I hope Ivan got his money back."

"Were you aware that Cartwright killed her as well as his secretary?" Liam asked.

Gareth looked startled for a moment then began to laugh.

"What's so funny?" Mark growled.

"Sorry, inside joke."

"Share with the class," Liam said.

"Kenneth always thought of himself as a lady killer. Guess he decided to take that more literally."

"You don't seem too upset," Mark noted.

Gareth shrugged. "Why should I cry over a stripper?"

"Because she was a human being?" Liam said a bit heatedly.

Mark held up a hand. "It's okay, Liam. Gareth here prefers men."

"What! I do not. Who told you that?" Gareth asked, the smirk leaving his face.

"I thought it was pretty common knowledge," Mark said. "After all, several people saw you hitting on Ivan all throughout the party."

"I wasn't hitting on him!" Gareth said heatedly.

"That's what it looked like to everyone else," Mark said, pushing to get further under the other guy's skin.

"I'm a salesman. I was just schmoozing the guy."

"Uh huh. And exactly what were you trying to sell him? Yourself?"

Gareth looked furious.

"Hey, relax," Liam said. "We understand. He's a good-looking guy, plenty of money. He'd be a real catch for you."

"I was trying to score an invite to the big gala this weekend. I was after his connections, not him or his money," Gareth snapped.

"And what connections would those be?"

"Powerful ones. The kind that make or break careers."

"So you were hoping he'd introduce you to what, his country club pals?" Mark asked sarcastically.

"I'd never expect someone like you to understand," Gareth said dismissively.

Mark had had his fill of snobs for the week. He grabbed Gareth by the front of his shirt. "So, explain it to me, real slow," he growled.

A look of fear shot into Gareth's eyes. Like most blowhards he was all talk and no bite. His eyes flicked to Liam.

"Liam, why don't you go take a walk around the block," Mark suggested in as menacing a voice as he could summon.

"Sounds good. I could use some fresh air. Plus, you know how I hate having to wash blood out of my clothes," Liam said nonchalantly.

"What?" Gareth asked as the color drained from his face.

"You heard the man," Mark said, yanking Gareth closer.

"Just try not to dismember this one. The paperwork's murder on those," Liam said as he headed for the door.

"No promises," Mark called after him.

In front of him Gareth was beginning to sweat profusely.

"You've got something to say? Mark asked.

"Please, don't… these guys, they don't mess around."

"Well, I'm not exactly a boy scout," Mark growled. "I assume these guys are going to be at the party?"

Gareth nodded. "A couple of them. Ivan said he'd introduce me."

"In exchange for what?"

"For not telling anyone that he and Ken had to drive Leo home. The man was totally wasted."

"Why did Ivan care if anyone knew he took Leo home?" Mark asked, thoughts racing ahead to possible answers.

"I don't know. The others left before me, and Leo was passed out drunk. The party broke up and they decided to drive him home. They said to keep quiet so it wouldn't hurt his reputation."

"Did you see them get him into the car?"

"No, I left like a minute before they did. I didn't want to have to help haul him out or anything."

"Why not?"

"I didn't want him waking up and puking on my new suit. It was expensive."

Liam was waiting, his hand on the doorknob, listening to every word.

"More expensive than you could really afford?" Mark guessed.

Gareth nodded.

"All to impress Ivan and his business friends?" Mark pushed.

Gareth nodded again.

"When did the stripper leave the party?"

"I don't know, early, not long after she got there."

"And did anyone else leave the room around the same time."

"I – I don't know."

"Think!" Mark hissed.

"Ivan and Ken, they were gone for a couple of minutes. I thought they were trying to find her."

"Anyone else?"

"No."

"What about Leo?"

"He was out cold. The guy can't hold his liquor."

"Did the stripper drink anything?"

"I don't know. I think so. I remember Ivan offered her a drink when he introduced her," Gareth said, beginning to whine.

Mark exchanged a quick glance with Liam who nodded. Mark abruptly let go of Gareth and stood up.

"Don't leave town. We'll be in touch," he said.

Gareth nodded, eyes wide and frightened.

Moments later Mark and Liam were back outside and in the car.

"You thinking what I'm thinking?" Mark asked.

"That Ivan, Ken, or both killed the stripper then took advantage of Leo's state and managed to get his fingerprints all over her and her things?"

"That's exactly what I'm thinking."

~

"Dinner is in half an hour," Joseph called from the kitchen when Jeremiah made it to the house after work.

He'd had to stay a few extra minutes to finish up a few things but he knew that Cindy and Geanie had already made it back safe.

"Sounds good," Jeremiah said before heading to the stairs.

Upstairs Jeremiah quickly changed into more comfortable clothes. He glanced around the guest room. He was using the same bedroom at Joseph's that he had before.

"Home away from home," he muttered. He opened the door, preparing to leave.

Downstairs he heard Captain bark sharply followed almost immediately by Clarice and Buster joining in. The room gave a sudden jolt.

"Earthquake!" he heard someone shout from downstairs as Jeremiah grabbed the door frame and braced himself.

Seconds later it was over. He'd been through several earthquakes since he moved to California and even the small ones still startled him.

He turned and saw that the room appeared to be fine. A pen on the nightstand had fallen on the floor and was rolling underneath the piece of furniture. A picture on one wall was a little crooked and otherwise everything else seemed untouched.

Jeremiah went over, got down and reached under the nightstand, feeling for the pen. He leaned down further so he could see under the nightstand and then he froze. There, underneath his nightstand, was a tiny listening device.

His room was bugged.

17

Cindy didn't like the look on Jeremiah's face when he came into the kitchen. Even though he smiled when he saw her she could tell that there was something wrong.

"Is everything okay?" she asked.

"Fine. I just need to pick up something at home."

"I'll go with you," Mark volunteered.

"No," Jeremiah said, a little too forcefully.

Mark glanced at Cindy and she could tell he was debating what to say.

Jeremiah forced a smile. "I'll be faster if I go by myself. I promise, I'll be right back," he said.

Mark's eyes narrowed to slits. "Don't suppose I can-"

"No, you can't," Jeremiah said, interrupting him.

He leaned over and kissed Cindy.

"I'll be right back," he said softly.

She nodded, wishing he would tell her what was going on. Clearly he wasn't ready to share, though. She watched as he headed toward the front door with a lump in her throat.

"Who's ready for my world famous fajitas?" Joseph asked cheerily.

"What makes them world famous?" Mark asked, grabbing a seat at the counter.

"I've won a few cooking contests with them all over the world," Joseph said with a straight face.

Mark's eyes bulged out and Joseph began to chuckle.

Geanie rolled her eyes. "They're world famous because he brags about them to anyone who will listen."

"Just like Mark with his barbeque," Traci chimed in.

"Hey, I make great barbeque. You guys know, you had it on the Fourth of July. And you had seconds and thirds. Well, most of you," he said, glancing at Cindy.

"It was delicious," Joseph said. "And so is this."

He put several sizzling hot plates down and the aroma of cooked meats and onions filled the air. They all grabbed plates and tortillas and started to eat.

A couple of minutes later Joseph's phone rang and he answered.

"Hello? Yes. Yes. No. No. Yes, please. Okay."

He hung up and Geanie stared at him, clearly waiting for him to explain who he'd just been talking to. She finally said, "Well?"

"Just a call regarding the security system, nothing to stress about," he said.

His answer seemed odd to Cindy and from the look on Geanie's face it clearly sounded strange to her as well. Joseph shrugged and Geanie went back to eating her fajitas.

~

Jeremiah hung up the phone. He'd called Joseph to ask him if the surveillance equipment was part of his home security. As expected the other man had confirmed that it was not and he had no idea how it might have gotten there. He'd also given Jeremiah his blessing to check over the entire house once he got back with some equipment. He'd told Joseph to only use yes or no answers so as not to upset everyone there. There was no sense in raising the alarm until he knew exactly what he was dealing with.

He had no way of knowing how long the listening device had been in place or whether the entire house was bugged or just certain areas. It was a huge mansion with most rooms seeing little to no usage in the average course of things. If whoever had planted those devices was even remotely familiar with Joseph, Geanie, and their frequent guests they would have planted them in the most high traffic areas. The best rooms to do surveillance on would be the living room and the kitchen. However, the presence of one of the devices in his room was proof that the master bedroom and the most frequently used guest bedrooms could all be impacted as well.

How long they'd been in place and which country had manufactured them would go a long way to helping figure out who might be behind them. If it was a recent invasion of privacy, then the best thing to do would be to leave the devices in place but set up masking in the rooms when people wanted to talk. That way it would take longer for whoever had planted them to become suspicious and make their next move. Just destroying them guaranteed a fast, unpredictable response.

Of course, there was a chance the devices had been there for a while and had nothing to do with recent events. From what he'd seen of the one, though, he'd be willing to bet this wasn't part of any criminal enterprise to rob Joseph or get business secrets out of him.

He'd like to think Martin would have warned him if the C.I.A. was behind it, but that kind of warning was highly unlikely. If it was his agency listening in then they had a reason they were trying to do it clandestinely. Given that

Martin knew who Jeremiah was now he couldn't think of another reason why the agency might be spying on Joseph or any of the rest of them.

What really worried him was the thought that it was linked to someone from his past, perhaps a former operative for another country. While it was not impossible that it was put there by a terrorist cell, it was more unlikely. They didn't usually care to know that much about their targets. They were more likely to just want intelligence about where their target was going to be so they might study flight paths and daily movement. That way when they struck they would be reasonably certain they would kill their target with whatever bomb or other weapon they planned to use.

The kind of detailed analysis, background information, and intelligence gathering suggested by the listening device was much more likely to be used by a current or former intelligence operative. Someone who had the time and the patience to sift through the data to discover what the other side knew and what plans they were making.

It was lucky that he had even found the bug. Some models couldn't even be detected by equipment designed to find them if they were in passive mode, not actively broadcasting. To help him clear the rooms he'd have to have someone talking while he swept so that any hidden devices wouldn't be on standby waiting for activity.

Due to the size of the mansion, it would be a waste of his time and energy to search the entire place from top to bottom. Even if he did there was no guarantee that he would find everything. His best bet was to thoroughly go over the few rooms that did have high traffic, the ones where they were likely to be having conversations in for the next few days.

It was time to hide a few weapons at the mansion. He should have done it ages ago. Better to have them and not need them.

He just hoped that whatever was going on they could clear it up before Cindy's family arrived. Somehow, though, he doubted that he'd be that lucky.

~

They were just finishing their meal when Jeremiah returned. Cindy wrapped her arms around him as he came up beside her.

"Everything okay?" she asked.

He shook his head, but didn't say anything. Instead he handed her a piece of paper. She looked at it and saw what he had written on it.

> I found a listening device in the bedroom upstairs. I need to check for more. While I do please continue to talk and act normally, but don't say anything important. Pass it on.

Cindy felt the blood drain from her cheeks. She handed the piece of paper to Mark who took it and began to read silently.

"Dinner looks fantastic Joseph. It always amazes me what a great cook you are."

The rest were looking at her strangely, but they'd know soon enough what was going on. Joseph said something about cooking, but she missed his meaning because she was too busy watching Jeremiah.

A minute later the note had been around the whole table and she could see that everyone else looked as nervous as she felt. They all managed to keep up idle chatter, though, while Jeremiah went through the kitchen checking everything, including the light fixtures and the air vents. He moved so silently she couldn't even hear him.

Once they had finished eating Jeremiah signaled everyone to move into the living room which he then proceeded to check thoroughly. After what seemed like an eternity he sat down on the couch next to her.

"This room is clear," he said.

"And the kitchen?" Joseph asked.

Jeremiah shook his head. "I have a few other rooms to check but for right now it's safe to talk in here."

"Who planted listening devices in our house?" Geanie asked.

"I don't know that yet, but I intend to find out," Jeremiah assured her. "Until I do we should all be careful about what we say."

"But it's okay to speak in this room?" Traci confirmed.

"Yes."

They all stared at each other for a moment. Cindy didn't know if they were all as lost for words as she was or if everyone was afraid that it really wasn't okay to speak normally.

"Well, this day just keeps getting better and better," Mark muttered.

"What happened?" Jeremiah asked.

"I had an unpleasant run-in with the would be Mrs. Cartwright. Awful woman."

"Amen to that," Geanie said.

"It's no exaggeration to say that she'd like to see Cindy dead," Mark added.

Jeremiah curled his lip in anger and there was so much menace on his face that Cindy felt a chill. She laid a hand on his arm. "It's okay," she said softly. "You can't kill everyone who doesn't like me."

"Sure I could. Besides, the list is small, it would only take a few minutes."

Cindy stared at Jeremiah in consternation. She wasn't sure he was joking. He looked thoroughly angry.

"So, is she the one trying to kill Cindy?" Joseph asked.

"I'm still not one hundred percent sure that someone is after Cindy. However, if, as we suspect, someone is I don't think it was her. As much as I'd love to throw her in jail for an eternity."

"Besides her who stands to benefit in some way from killing Leo and Beau and trying to kill Cindy? I mean, I guess there's a chance that Cartwright could be acquitted if all the witnesses against him go missing, but could he really orchestrate something like that from prison?" Traci asked.

"It depends on what kind of friends he has and what they'd be willing to do for him. I'd wager he doesn't have that kind of power himself, but his best man, Ivan, is just the kind of cocky, arrogant son of a … gun who might try to pull something like that off."

"So, what do we know about Ivan?" Jeremiah asked.

"Besides the fact that he's a smug piece of work with a 'you can't touch me' attitude? Not as much as I would like," Mark admitted. "I do know that he has some sort of money or influence. Whatever it was it was enough to have

Gareth, the salesman, fawning over him at the party. I also know he's pretty versed on his rights. There's no way he's going to talk willingly. Not to me."

"Then to who?" Cindy asked.

"All that man respects is power. That was pretty clear to me."

"So, maybe we find someone he would talk to," Cindy said.

Mark gave a short bitter laugh. "Good luck pulling that one off."

"Maybe a social setting would make him more relaxed, more likely to slip up," Traci said.

"I don't think the man will come over for tea no matter how politely I invite him," Mark said.

"Maybe not tea, but perhaps something else?" Geanie suggested.

"The only place I know he's going to be is that charity gala thing Friday night. Apparently there will be a few people there Gareth was hoping he'd introduce him to."

"What you need is to catch him off his guard, get him talking," Jeremiah said.

"If only I had a way to get someone into that party," Mark chafed. "I gather it is invitation only, though, very exclusive."

"So, what you need is someone who's been invited," Joseph said.

"Yeah."

"A guy you know who you could trust who could move among these men with ease."

"Exactly," Mark said.

"Someone they don't know and wouldn't associate with you or the police," Joseph continued.

"That's exactly what I need," Mark said with a sigh. "I'd have better luck finding a unicorn."

Joseph raised an eyebrow. "I don't think I'm that rare a creature."

Mark looked at him sharply. "What?"

Joseph smiled. "I've been invited to that gala."

"How?"

"I'm guessing it has something to do with the fact that he's rich," Jeremiah interposed.

"And I give a lot to charity," Joseph added. "I wasn't planning on going, but I think I could be persuaded to change my mind."

Mark blinked rapidly as he took it all in. "Can you get your hands on one of those white tie outfits in time?"

Joseph glanced at Geanie. "I think he just insulted me."

Geanie smirked. "I think we can find something appropriate in his closet. We will make a grand showing."

"Oh no, you're not going," Mark said.

"Why?" she asked, clearly startled.

"These guys haven't shown the greatest respect for women. Besides, if they are up to something devious Joseph will be more approachable if he's alone."

"That's true," Jeremiah said quickly.

"I don't like the idea of him talking to murderers by himself," Geanie said.

"He won't be alone. I'll have a wire on him. If anything goes wrong we can pull him out in seconds," Mark said.

"It will be fine," Joseph said, smiling reassuringly at Geanie. "I'll just be going to another boring party and hoping that somebody propositions me."

Jeremiah coughed and Mark smirked. Cindy tried so hard to hold in a laugh. Geanie's expression was priceless.

"Maybe you want to rethink that," Traci suggested, clearly struggling not to laugh as well.

"Wait, that didn't come out the way I meant," Joseph said quickly.

"I should hope not," Geanie said.

"At any rate, it will be a large party. The only thing the bad guys can do is talk to me."

Cindy wasn't entirely sure that was true, and from the expression on his face neither was Mark, but he clearly didn't want to worry Geanie.

She glanced at Jeremiah. After the moment of levity he was again scowling. She wasn't sure which of all the pressing matters was weighing on him heaviest. Suddenly he stood, looking like a man on a mission. He reached down and took her hand.

"What is it?" she asked.

"While everyone is working out the logistics here I think it's past time we went to your bedroom."

Chapter 18

"What?" Cindy asked, looking up at Jeremiah with her eyes dilating slightly.

"I need to check it for bugs," he said, realizing belatedly how what he'd said must have sounded.

"Sure you do," Mark teased.

It was good that the detective was in the mood to tease, but Jeremiah could have smacked him for his timing.

"Oh, of course," Cindy said, hastily standing up.

"We'll check everyone else's as well," Jeremiah said, glancing around the room.

"How very Goldilocks," Traci said, barely suppressing a giggle. "Do tell us which one has a bed that's just right."

"Traci!" Cindy burst out.

And just like that everyone was laughing. Traci was clutching her stomach and she pointed at Cindy. "You should see your face!"

"You're bright red," Geanie added, laughing even harder than Traci.

"Thanks, guys," Cindy said sarcastically.

~

Cindy was flushed and Jeremiah looked distinctly uncomfortable. Mark felt a little sorry for both of them, but not sorry enough to keep from laughing along with the others.

"Tell you what, we'll work on figuring out who's trying to listen in on our conversations," Jeremiah said, "and you guys figure out what to do about Ivan and the party."

"I'm still struggling to understand why you're targeting Ivan," Traci said to Mark.

"Because I think he might have sent the man who killed Leo and Beau," Mark explained.

"So, Ivan's motivation is what? Get his friend out of prison?"

"That's motivation enough for some," Mark said.

"So, are we assuming that Cartwright killed both women?"

"It's the cleanest answer," Mark said.

"Which doesn't necessarily make it the right one," Traci pointed out.

"Thanks, hon," he said sarcastically.

She shrugged, clearly not bothered. "I'm just saying sometimes things are… complicated. Even when it comes to murder."

"True, but I'm really hoping in this instance it's not."

"Bad guy kills a woman, likes it, kills another, and is what, on his way to becoming a serial killer when he gets caught?" Joseph asked.

"It's not like we haven't had serial killers in Pine Springs before," Cindy said.

Jeremiah tugged on her hand and led her from the room.

"And then the bad guy's best buddy tries to free him. I can see that," Geanie said.

"That's pretty far to go for a friend," Joseph commented.

Geanie asked, "What, you mean all of you wouldn't plan to help set me free if I went on a murder spree?"

"You are kidding, right?" Mark asked.

"No, I think it's a valid question," Geanie said. "How far would Cartwright's friends go? I mean, would my friends go that far?" she asked, glancing around at the rest of them.

Mark glanced at Traci. "Is this some weird girl test?" he asked.

Traci punched him in the arm. "It's not a girl test. I think it's a valid question. How far would any of us go to protect the others?"

The question lingered in the air and they all grew silent. The mood which a few minutes before had been playful suddenly felt somber, dark. Mark didn't like the direction things had taken.

"Let's not go down that rabbit hole," he said.

"Why not?" Geanie asked. "You want us to believe that Ivan went down that rabbit hole for his best friend."

"Yeah, but Ivan isn't exactly a law-abiding, upstanding citizen," Mark said.

"How do you know?" Joseph asked. "All you really know about him is that he's arrogant and that he prizes money and power. That doesn't make him a criminal. At best he's an ambitious, successful businessman."

Mark felt like he had inadvertently stepped on a landmine. "Look, there's something about the guy. He's slimy. I feel it in my gut."

"Well, last I checked slimy wasn't a crime," Traci said.

"Whose side are you on?" he asked.

"Yours, babe, always," she said. "But it's possible this man just rubbed you the wrong way and you are ascribing villainy to him when he just irritates you."

"You've never questioned my hunches before," he said, irritation flooding him.

~

Once they left the living room Cindy could no longer hear what the others were saying. That was probably just as well since the kitchen apparently had a listening device in it. If she couldn't hear them outside the living room odds were their mysterious stalker couldn't either.

Jeremiah held her hand as they walked upstairs.

"You okay?" he asked.

"I guess. It's just been… a lot," she said, not really wanting to elaborate in case someone else could hear.

"You're handling things really well."

"Thanks."

They made it in her room and she sat down on the bed while Jeremiah started walking around checking everything.

"Looking forward to taking your parents to The Zone?" he asked.

"It should be fun. Although I expect Kyle to want to go on all the things in the Extreme Zone area, like the bungee jumping and ziplining. I don't see Mom or Dad wanting to join in on that."

"How about you?"

She snorted. "Surely you're joking."

"I'll go with Kyle if you want."

"Yes, because the two of you standing on top of a tiny platform where one of you could push the other off is my idea of a good time."

"I promise not to kill him."

"Uh huh," Cindy said.

"I can't guarantee I won't scare him," he said, sounding slightly amused.

Cindy couldn't help but laugh at that a little bit. "I bet there's a lot of people that would pay good money to see that."

"Maybe I can sell the footage to the Escape Channel and get enough for it that I can take you on a really fantastic honeymoon."

Her breath caught in her throat. "Oh."

"Yup, maybe just scare him a little bit. And then throw a big party, a festival in honor of the occasion."

"Oh no!"

"What's wrong?" Jeremiah asked sharply.

"I just realized you didn't get to celebrate yesterday, Israel Independence, right?"

"Yom Ha'atzmaut, yes. Everyone who wanted to celebrate publicly went over to show support for the synagogue that burned on Monday."

"Shouldn't you have been there?" she asked, distressed that he'd been missing that.

"No, it was fine. I already expressed my support and sympathy to the rabbi."

"But there's that other holiday coming up, the one that's on the same day as Mother's Day. What are you going to do?"

"Figure out a way to compromise and celebrate both. We're both going to have to get used to that and it's a fine time to start."

"Do you want me to actually participate?"

"If you wish."

She tucked her knees up and wrapped her arms around them. "That's something we haven't really discussed. What are the duties of a rabbi's wife?"

"Much the same as a pastor's wife, I imagine," Jeremiah said.

"I guess I should start learning more about… everything," she said.

"Probably a good idea. And, your room is clear."

"That's a relief," she said, feeling like a weight had been lifted."

"Yes. Come on, we've got a few more rooms to check."

~

That night Jeremiah struggled to fall asleep. The only two bugs he'd found had been the one in his room and the one in the kitchen. He'd left them both in place. The fact that of all the bedrooms only his was bugged told him that whoever had left the listening devices was targeting him and not Joseph or Geanie. That did little to help him fall asleep.

He also kept going over the different conversations of the evening. It would be amazing if Cindy decided to actively participate in the synagogue. There was a lot he'd have to teach her. On the other hand, he was sure there was still a lot she needed to teach him about her faith.

He was looking forward to the challenge. He just prayed that they survived long enough to enjoy it.

~

Friday night had finally arrived. Mark, Jeremiah, and Joseph were seated in the back of a limousine on the way to the charity gala. Joseph was wearing a wire so that Mark and Jeremiah could hear everything that happened while Joseph was inside.

Ordinarily this was not the type of thing Mark would have invited a civilian to, but if things went well they might need Jeremiah there. It didn't hurt that both Mark and Liam were in no shape to do any sprinting or tackling if it was called for. So, Liam was stuck driving the limo and Mark had drafted the rabbi instead to help monitor Joseph's conversations.

Not that he'd had to twist Jeremiah's arm very hard. The man was clearly as concerned for Joseph's well-being as he was. Plus, Mark was fairly certain that Jeremiah was eager to think about anything except his future in-laws' pending arrival. It should make for an interesting night.

So long as Joseph didn't get killed.

"Are you sure you're up for this?" Mark asked. "It's going to require a lot of acting. Undercover work is challenging. You'll need to blend in, but not tip your hand." He was feeling worse about it with every word he uttered. "You know what, this is a bad idea, we'll get someone else."

"I've been around these types of people since I was born. I think I know how to act like one of them," Joseph said calmly.

"It's just I'm worried. You're too nice and they're… not."

And then something seemed to come over Joseph. He straightened his shoulders slightly and he seemed larger somehow, like he was filling the space around him. When he spoke there was a cold, haughty sound in his voice. "Don't just sit there gawking. Make yourself useful. Fix me a beverage and remember to bring my car around at ten sharp. I don't want to stay any longer than I have to."

"What?" Mark asked, startled.

Joseph rolled his eyes. "Dear heavens, the man is deaf. Or an idiot. Which one is it?" He paused and then continued in slow, loud tones, "Hello? Do you understand me? I can see by your vacant stare that you do not."

"What are you playing at?" Mark growled.

"*Mr.* Walters, it has become altogether clear to me that you wouldn't know the first thing about trying to blend in with this crowd. As soon as this vehicle stops I will get out and you can run along and do… whatever it is your type does."

Joseph dismissed him with the wave of a hand. Mark could feel the anger roiling in him. "That's not funny."

Joseph stared at him in clear disdain for several seconds. Then, suddenly, his features softened again. "No, no it's not," he said. "I've seen the game played my whole life. Who has more money and can demonstrate it easier. Who has power and what is the pecking order. Who is more arrogant, more in control, better than everyone else. Just because I don't play the games doesn't mean I don't know how they're played… and how to win. You could walk into a store wearing an expensive suit. I could walk in wearing ratty jeans and a torn T-shirt. And I can guarantee you that if I chose, every salesperson there would ignore you and head straight for me. It's not how you look, it's the confidence, the arrogance you exude. You can walk into a Ferrari dealership looking like a bum, but if you believe in your gut that you can buy and sell every man there ten times over, they will crawl on their bellies to you."

"I have to admit you're starting to scare me a bit."

"You should be scared. There are two types of people that attend these kinds of functions. Those who are grateful for what they have and genuinely want to give back and those who want to manipulate and use as many people as they possibly can in the time they have."

"How much money do you actually have?" Mark asked in wonder.

Joseph smiled and something dark crept into it. "Enough to buy and sell everyone in that room ten times over."

"I'm thinking we should all be very grateful that you're a good guy."

"Yes, you should. Now, let's go, I don't have all night to devote to this little escapade."

"I kind of hate you right now, no offense."

Joseph smirked. "You say that as though you think it should have some impact on me."

"Okay, we need to do this fast. I can't take much more of this Joseph," Mark said.

"You know what they say, be careful what you wish for. By the way, I'd check your mortgage balance if I were you," Joseph said, punching a few things on his phone before pocketing it.

"Why?" Mark asked.

"It's not good to be carrying that much debt when you have two infants to take care of."

"That's none of your-"

"Business? Actually it is. I own the company that holds your loan. Don't worry, though, I just paid it in full for you. You're welcome." Joseph opened the door and got out of the limo.

Mark stood there gaping at Joseph's back as the man stalked toward the building. He turned to Jeremiah who had a look of respect on his face. "What was that?"

"I'd call it a very important object lesson. Never, ever piss off Joseph."

"I'm not sure who that was, but that wasn't Joseph," Mark said.

"Which is a good thing for us at the moment," Jeremiah pointed out.

The limo pulled away from the curb and drove around the block to park behind the building. Jeremiah and Mark wore headphones so they could hear the chatter around Joseph and his occasional response to someone as he made his way inside.

"It's weird. I always knew Joseph was rich, but the last few days I'm getting an idea that he has a lot more money than he lets on," Mark said.

"Does that bother you?" Jeremiah asked.

"No, it's just… I don't know. You don't expect the super rich to be real people. I guess it just kind of freaks me out a little. I like Joseph just the way he is."

Jeremiah chuckled. "And he's been super rich his entire life. I don't think he's going to suddenly change now."

"He better not."

"You've been acting strangely all week," Jeremiah noted.

"I guess. That bank up in Sacramento kind of freaked me out. It was like I was in another country or something," Mark admitted. "Then on top of that I find out that Not Paul had a kid, yet another thing I didn't know about him.

Then I find out that Joseph's probably got some sort of vault at that bank. I'm starting to wonder if I really know the truth about anyone in my life. And if not, what kind of terrible detective does that make me?"

"You know the truth about me."

"Yeah, but how do I know that's it, that you won't lay another bombshell on me one of these days?" Mark asked.

Jeremiah looked at him as though the rabbi thought he'd lost his mind. "Because clearly I could have a secret that's more earth-shattering than that one."

"You never know."

"I think you've gotten a little paranoid."

"Wouldn't you?" Mark demanded.

"You know what they say, it's not paranoia if people really are out to get you."

Something in Jeremiah's tone of voice gave Mark pause. He studied the other man closely, but as usual could read nothing in his expression.

"Is something going on I should know about?" Mark asked.

Jeremiah was silent for long enough that Mark began to squirm. Finally, the other man said, "Hopefully not."

"Yes, that sounds very reassuring," Mark said, letting the sarcasm drip from his voice. "Are you talking about actual bad guys or the impending arrival of Cindy's family?"

"Let's say both."

"Kyle still have hard feelings for you?"

"As near as I can tell."

"Any indication about Cindy's parents?"

Jeremiah shrugged. "With her mother, who knows."

"And her father?"

"The man is smart… smart enough to have guessed that there's more to me than meets the eye."

"Maybe that will go in your favor," Mark suggested.

Jeremiah actually laughed out loud. "Somehow I doubt that."

Mark knew that Jeremiah had been cut off from his own family back in Israel. It would be rough if Cindy's family rejected him as well. He hoped for his friend's sake that wasn't the case. He tried to think of something reassuring to say. Before he could, though, a voice came through loud and clear on the receiver.

"Mr. Coulter, I don't believe we've met. My name is Ivan."

Mark felt himself tense up. This was it. He was starting to think this was foolish. He didn't know what he expected Joseph to get out of the man. After all, it wasn't like Ivan was likely to confess to murder to a stranger at a party.

"Hello, Ivan," Joseph said, his tone haughty.

"How are you enjoying the gala?"

Joseph sighed heavily. "I honestly don't know why I even bother coming to these things sometimes. The company and the conversation are always terribly dull."

"Well, maybe I can liven things up a bit for you."

"I'm not sure how," Joseph said, sounding bored and unimpressed.

"You seem to me a man who could use a little more adventure in his life, who would enjoy socializing with like-minded individuals."

"I'm already a member of a dozen country clubs and I don't visit any of them more than twice a year," Joseph said.

Ivan chuckled. "I'm not trying to sell you on a country club. The group I represent is much more... discriminating."

"I'm sure it is. And what small fortune is the privilege of joining going to cost me?" Joseph asked sarcastically.

"No money. What we're offering can't be bought, at any price," Ivan said.

There was a pause and Mark found himself leaning closer to the receiver and holding his breath.

"What exactly is it you're offering?" Joseph asked, a hint of interest in his voice.

"Fellowship with other powerful people with similar views."

"And this fellowship won't cost me anything?"

"Not monetarily," Ivan said. "I think we can all agree that past a certain point money becomes somewhat meaningless. Other things take on a much greater importance. Things like camaraderie, loyalty, influence. Interested?"

"Maybe."

"Here's my card. Please call me anytime and we can discuss this further, more privately," Ivan said.

"Alright."

"Have a great rest of your night. I look forward to hearing from you."

Mark sat back and let out his breath. He could hear Joseph still moving around, greeting people. He wasn't due to come out for a while, but hopefully he would make an exit soon. "What on earth do you think that was about?"

"Sounds like he wants Joseph to join some sort of organization. Probably a secret one," Jeremiah said.

"I don't know what I was expecting, but that wasn't it," Mark said.

"At least it's something."

"Yeah, but it means I'm going to have to keep putting Joseph in danger if I want to pursue this angle."

"Do you have any other direction you can come at Ivan from?" Jeremiah asked.

"Not at this point," Mark admitted.

"Well, then we'll just have to deal with it."

Mark passed a hand through his hair. "Things are just going to get weirder aren't they?"

"Probably."

"And Cindy's folks show up tomorrow. What are you going to do?"

Jeremiah sighed. "I'll just have to deal with that, too."

"You, bartender, I'll have something strong and make it a double," Joseph said suddenly and loudly enough to startle Mark.

"What's he doing?" Mark hissed. "Does he even drink?"

Jeremiah shrugged.

"Come on Joseph, stay in character. Just leave before you do something that will get you in trouble," Mark said anxiously.

"He can't hear you, you know," Liam said from the front of the limo.

"I should have made him wear an earbud," Mark chafed.

"So you could really distract him and blow his cover?" Jeremiah asked.

"Thanks a lot," Mark said sarcastically.

Suddenly they could hear Ivan's voice, low and menacing. "I'd kill to get what you have."

19

"That's Ivan," Mark said, heart beginning to pound. "What's he doing? We need to get Joseph out of there now."

Mark's hand flew to the door but Jeremiah stopped him with a hand on his arm. "Wait, let's see where this is going."

"Are you crazy?"

"No. Like you said, it's a crowded place and he has no reason to suspect Joseph. Let's see where he's going with this."

"And what exactly is it you would kill for," Joseph asked calmly.

"A stiff drink," Ivan said with a laugh.

Mark slumped back in his chair. Jeremiah was right. It's just that the whole thing was nerve-wracking. It was all made the worse by the fact that Joseph was not only a civilian but also one of his best friends. Not to mention that Traci would kill him if something happened to one of her go-to babysitters.

"I'm so over this party," Joseph said. He sounded completely bored. "I feel like I can't stand another fundraiser. What was this one for again? Widows? Orphans?"

"Something like that," Ivan said with a sharp laugh. "I'll have whatever he's having."

Mark couldn't take much more of this. "What is he doing? He's made contact, now it's time to get out. We've got to pull him out of there."

"Give it a minute. Joseph's a pretty shrewd guy. Let him play this out," Jeremiah said.

"If he gets killed it's on your head, not mine," Mark said fervently.

"My... lovely... wife probably wishes she was a widow," Joseph said with a touch of dark humor.

"I'm sure that's not the case," Ivan said.

"Don't worry, I can assure you the feeling is absolutely mutual. Oh, the things I could do if I didn't have her to worry about."

Mark couldn't help but feel offended for Geanie even though he knew the entire thing was an act. He wished he knew where Joseph was going with all of this.

"There's always divorce," Ivan said. "It's made a free man out of many poor sods."

"That's just the problem. I'm not poor."

"No prenup?" Ivan asked, clearly feigning sympathy.

"That's right. I believe I had some romantic notion at the time about love lasting forever. Hard to imagine I was ever that naïve."

"Well, there are always other ways," Ivan said.

Mark exchanged a glance with Jeremiah.

Joseph laughed bitterly. "If you have suggestions I'd love to hear them."

There was a pause and Mark realized he was holding his breath as he waited for an answer.

"I just might. Give me a call and I'll tell you all about them," Ivan said at last.

"Dang!" Mark said, slumping in his seat. "For a moment there I thought we had him."

"Joseph has him. He's just not going to bite in public," Jeremiah said. "Ivan hasn't made it this far by being an idiot."

"You're right."

"You know what? I just might," Joseph said, a tiny bit of intrigue in his voice.

"He's really good at this," Jeremiah said. "He's making Ivan work to capture his interest. That way Ivan will think he's a master at manipulation when really Joseph is."

"There's a frightening thought," Mark said.

"Guys like us should stick together," Ivan said smoothly.

There was the sound of ice cubes tinkling in glasses.

"To your future freedom," Ivan said. "Talk to you later."

There was some background noise as it sounded like Joseph was on the move again.

"You don't think he really paid off my house, do you?" Mark asked.

"I wouldn't assume anything right at the moment."

In the front of the limo Liam's phone rang. Through his headphones Mark could hear Joseph talking to his partner.

"Bring the car around. I'm leaving," Joseph said.

Liam started up the car and two minutes later Joseph was getting inside. As soon as his door was closed Liam drove off and Mark shook his head at Joseph.

"What? Didn't I do enough?" Joseph asked.

"Actually, I thought you went a bit overboard," Mark said.

"You were perfect," Jeremiah said.

"So, you'll call him tomorrow," Mark said.

"No," Jeremiah and Joseph said in unison.

"Excuse me?" Mark asked.

"I'd come off as too eager. The best thing would be to wait until Tuesday or Wednesday to call."

Mark scowled. "The best thing is to get a confession and get this guy off the streets before he or someone else takes another shot at killing Cindy or me for that matter."

"Then Sunday. I can fake a fight with my wife that has driven me to distraction," Joseph said. "Any sooner and it will seem suspicious to him."

"Agreed," Jeremiah said.

"Last I checked I was in charge of this undercover mission," Mark said.

"Actually it's turned into more of a sting. And they're right. Too eager will scare this guy off," Liam chimed in from the front.

For a moment Mark seriously considered shutting the privacy window. "Traitor," he contented himself with grumbling instead.

~

As Jeremiah circled the airport the next morning he wondered exactly how he was going to deal with Cindy's family, particularly in light of all that had happened in the last few days. Cindy sat next to him. She'd been quiet for most of the ride and when he glanced at her now he could see the scowl on her face.

"You okay?" he asked.

"I'm fine," she said.

"You don't look fine. You look upset," he said.

"I'm not looking forward to being under the same roof with both Kyle and my mom," she said.

"Maybe it will be fun."

She snorted derisively.

"Maybe it won't be the end of the world," he amended. "And we get to go to The Zone, so that should be cool. I don't think we go often enough."

"That's true. I just wish everything weren't so unsettled. I mean, why do they have to be here when we're in the middle of a mystery?"

He thought about making a comment about when were they not in the middle of a mystery but decided against it. The humor would be lost on her at the moment and might even add to her stress.

Cindy's phone beeped.

"Dad just texted. They have their bags and are heading outside."

Jeremiah edged over into the right hand lane. He managed to pull up to the curb just as Don and Carol stepped through the doors of the terminal. He got out and grabbed the bags from Don.

"Thank you," Don said.

"You're welcome. It's good to see you again," Jeremiah said as he put them into the trunk.

Cindy got out of the car and gave both her parents a quick hug.

"Dad, Mom, you remember Jeremiah," she said.

"Not really," Carol answered in clipped tones.

Jeremiah winced inwardly. *So it begins.*

He slammed the trunk closed and turned with a smile. "Shall we?"

They all got in the car, and a minute later they were putting the airport behind them.

"What happened to your arm?" Don asked.

"I broke it," Cindy said.

"How?" Carol asked.

"It's a long story. I'll tell you later. I... fell... at home," Cindy said.

"This is the home we don't get to see?" Carol asked, suspicion heavy in her voice.

"Uh huh. So, like I said on the phone last night, we're all going to be staying at our friends' house. They have a mansion. You'll like it. It's huge," Cindy said brightly. "It's like a bit of a vacation for us all."

"I don't understand why we have to stay at a stranger's house," Carol said irritably.

"Just let it go," Don said softly.

Jeremiah was pretty certain that Cindy's mom never let anything go. Cindy probably got some of her tenacity from her. He should be grateful. Without that very quality Cindy would likely have given up on him long before.

"This doesn't have something to do with one of those silly mysteries you keep obsessing over, does it?" Carol asked.

Jeremiah almost lost control of the car. He risked a quick glance at Cindy who was pale and shaking.

"They're not silly, Carol. She does a great job catching killers and saving people," Don said.

"That's what police are for. I wish she could find some worthwhile hobby," the woman sniffed.

"I doubt the people she's helped feel that way," Don said softly.

"We have the whole day to do whatever you'd like. Kyle's not getting in until late. I figure we can go out to lunch as soon as we get your stuff dropped at the house," Cindy said, clearly trying to ignore the exchange between her parents. Her voice sounded a lot calmer than Jeremiah would have expected under the circumstances. She truly was a remarkable woman.

"That will be fine," Don said. "It will give us a chance to talk, get to know Jeremiah here a little better."

"I can't believe you got engaged to a man we don't even know," Carol burst out.

Several emotions collided within Jeremiah. He forced himself to take a deep breath as the thought of strangling the woman nearly overwhelmed him. When you'd lived a life like he had such thoughts were anything but harmless. He was going to need to keep his guard up so he didn't say or do anything he shouldn't.

"That's why you're here visiting, to get to know him," Cindy said doggedly.

"I myself am looking forward to getting to know you better," Jeremiah said, trying to help. "You both did such a fantastic job raising a smart, funny, kind woman. I'd like to thank you for that."

"We didn't do it for you," Carol sniffed.

Jeremiah grit his teeth. She wasn't going to make it easy on him. He forced a smile onto his face even though she couldn't see it. If she wanted to set herself up as an enemy combatant he could handle that. He just didn't want Cindy getting hurt in the crossfire.

He forced himself to take a deep breath. This was a job that called for more finesse than brute strength. He had infiltrated terrorist strongholds before. What was one more?

~

Mark was on pins and needles. It felt like everything had come down to a waiting game. He was waiting for Joseph to contact Ivan, for Cindy's parents and Kyle to show up, and for someone to make another move against Cindy or him. He was a witness to Cartwright's confession, too.

"You're awfully jumpy," Traci commented as they sat down with Joseph and Geanie for brunch. They were sitting in the living room instead of the kitchen where they usually ate just so they could speak freely.

"I can't help it. I've got a bad feeling."

"About what?" Geanie asked.

"Everything," he admitted. "Things have been too quiet, going too well."

"Um, hello?" Geanie said, scrunching her forehead up at him. "Cindy and Jeremiah were nearly killed in her house, someone is spying on us at our house, Cindy's arm is broken, two of Cindy's former coworkers are dead, you've been stabbed, Joseph has to try and trap a killer, Liam's still busted up, and to top it all off Cindy's crazy mom and her awful brother are invading today. Exactly how are things going well?"

Mark couldn't explain the sense of foreboding that he was feeling. Something in his gut told him that things were going to get darker. Much, much darker.

He shot a fearful glance at Traci who reached over and squeezed his hand.

"We'll get through it, no matter what," she said.

She was always his rock.

~

Cindy's nerves were stretched practically to the breaking point by the time they arrived at Joseph and Geanie's house. Her father whistled low as he got out of the car.

"You weren't kidding about it being a mansion," he said.

"It really is an amazing place," Cindy said, grateful that her dad was helping to fill the silence that was radiating from her mom.

Jeremiah moved around to the trunk. "I'll take your bags to your room while Cindy gives you the tour," he said.

"Are you sure you don't need a hand?" Don asked.

"No, thank you. I've got it," Jeremiah said, smiling at the older man. He pulled the luggage out of the trunk, closed it, and quickly headed inside.

Cindy turned to her parents. Her mom was scowling at her intently.

"I can't for the life of me figure out what you see in that man," Carol sniffed.

A thousand retorts ran through Cindy's mind and she struggled to keep from saying them. She took a deep breath and said, "I love him."

~

It didn't take a detective to figure out that something had gone horribly wrong on the ride from the airport. Mark was coming downstairs when the front door opened and Jeremiah walked in with a couple of suitcases. His face was cold, expressionless. He hadn't looked that bad since right after he came back from Israel.

Past the rabbi Mark could see Cindy and an older couple walking up to the door. None of them looked happy. They made it inside before Mark could say anything. He finished coming down the stairs.

"Dad, Mom, this is our friend, Detective Mark Walters," Cindy said. "Mark, these are my parents Don and Carol."

Mark suddenly struggled with what to say. Given how things were looking it certainly wasn't good to meet them. He was equally sure he didn't want to ask how things were going. It wasn't his house so he couldn't technically welcome them to it. He finally managed to get out a strangled, "Hello."

Don extended his hand and Mark shook it.

Joseph and Geanie emerged from the kitchen and walked over, much to Mark's relief. This was definitely a case of the more the merrier.

"Hello, welcome to our home," Joseph said warmly.

It was nice to have the normal Joseph back after what Mark had seen of undercover Joseph the night before.

"It's an impressive house," Don said, shaking his hand as well.

Joseph shrugged. "We enjoy having family and friends here. Cindy is certainly both in our eyes."

"Thank you," Don said.

Mark noticed that while Carol also shook hands with Joseph and Geanie, there was no warmth on her face. He hoped for all their sakes that she'd thaw out. Otherwise it was going to be a long few days.

~

Cindy was seething as she showed her parents their room upstairs. Jeremiah had already left their bags and vanished. She just prayed he hadn't heard what her mom said outside. She'd been so shocked by what her mother had said that she had barely managed to give a civil response.

It was going to be a miserable few days unless they found a way to turn this all around. Unfortunately their friends couldn't provide a buffer twenty-four hours a day. Although Geanie would probably try if she asked her to.

"It's a nice room," Don said with a smile.

"All the furniture in here is antiques," Cindy said.

"Very, very beautiful. Of course, it doesn't hold a candle to you," he said with a wink.

"Thanks, Dad," she said.

"Jeremiah is making you happy?" he asked.

"Yes," she said, blushing.

Her mom's scowl deepened. "I can see things are worse than I feared. I'm going to have to work fast," Carol said.

"To do what?" Cindy asked.

"To break the two of you up."

20

Cindy stared at her mom in horror. "That… that's why you came to visit?" she sputtered, barely able to get the words out.

"Why else?" Carol asked, raising an eyebrow.

"Come on, Carol," Don said. "Don't do this."

"Give me one good reason," Carol said, challenging him.

"He doesn't have to," Cindy said, anger welling up within her. "I'll give you three. Jeremiah makes me happy. I'm an adult and I can make my own decisions. And you're my mom and even if you don't respect my decisions I expect you to love me enough to want me to be happy. I should have known that would be too much to ask of you. Feel free to go back home. I don't need you here."

Shaking from head to toe Cindy stormed out of the room. She ran down the stairs and yanked open the front door. She stood there for a moment, wanting to get in a car and drive until she had left the pain far behind. She couldn't, though. She was under house arrest essentially until the whole Leo mess was resolved.

She slammed the door shut and headed to the living room where she collapsed onto one of the sofas. She screamed and punched one of the pillows, needing to do something.

"I feel sorry for that pillow. Whatever it did, though, I'm sure it deserved it."

She looked up and saw her dad standing in the doorway.

"Someone deserved it," she said, misery replacing her anger.

He walked over and sat down next to her. "Sweetheart, I think it's time you told me what's really going on. Don't worry, I won't tell your mother."

She didn't want to talk about it. All the grief and fear of the last few days came bubbling to the surface, though, and she could feel the tears starting to course down her cheeks.

"It's okay," he said, stroking her hair. "You know I won't judge."

"Someone I knew, someone I was trying to help was murdered in my house Tuesday," she said with a sob. "And I was there."

His eyes widened slightly, but he didn't say anything, just kept stroking her hair like he used to do when she was little and crying. She turned and buried her face in his shoulder and cried.

~

Somehow Jeremiah and Cindy's plans to take her parents out to lunch had gotten derailed. Judging from the look on Jeremiah's face Mark was pretty sure he didn't want to know what had happened. Cindy and her father were still in the living room. Her mother was upstairs. Jeremiah was in the kitchen with him, Joseph, Geanie, and Traci. He could tell that the others were feeling just as much at a loss as he was.

The doorbell rang and the five of them all went into the foyer. It was ridiculous, actually, but each one of them was somehow jumping at the chance to do *something*, even if it was just answer the door.

Geanie was the first one to it and she threw it open wide. A man was standing outside, bags in hand.

"I finished filming sooner than expected so I took an earlier flight," he said.

"Oh hey, look, Kyle's here," Mark said, sarcasm dusting his tone.

Jeremiah bit his lip. If there was anyone who disliked Cindy's brother as much as Mark did, it would be Jeremiah. At least Mark would never have to call the guy brother-in-law.

"Come in," Geanie said.

Kyle came in and dropped his bags in the entry as Geanie closed the door. Kyle glanced around and his eyes settled on Traci.

"Hi, Traci, good to see you," Kyle said with a smile.

"You're looking well," she said.

"Thank you."

"Would you mind if I got a selfie with you?" she asked.

"Not at all."

Mark tried not to roll his eyes as Traci moved over next to Kyle, camera at the ready. "I want to send it to my sister. She repeatedly tells the story of seeing Chuck Norris once in an airport."

"Wanting to one up her?" Kyle asked.

"You bet."

Traci held out her camera. At the last moment Kyle leaned in closer and kissed her cheek. Mark fought the urge to hit him for it.

"Perfect! Thanks," Traci gushed as she texted the picture.

"Amber's going to be over here before you know it," Mark warned.

Traci smirked. "Ah, but she doesn't know where we are. It's going to drive her crazy. And sent."

"Um, there's just one flaw in that plan."

"What's that?" she asked.

Mark grimaced. "I kinda already called their house and told her husband where we'd be in case they needed to know."

"You what?" Traci asked, eyes going wide.

"Yeah."

"Great. Now she's going to break every speeding law there is to get here," Traci said.

"I take it she's a fan?" Kyle asked with raised eyebrows.

"Little bit," Mark said.

"Well, should be an interesting few days. Although, I'm still not sure why we're here and not Cindy's house."

Mark noticed that Kyle was studiously avoiding looking at Jeremiah. In fact, he looked at everyone but the rabbi. No love lost either way it seemed.

Suddenly Carol seemed to come flying down the stairs. "There's my boy!" she shouted, her face positively glowing. She threw her arms around Kyle and hugged him tight. Mark saw Jeremiah scowl. He was guessing Cindy hadn't gotten so warm a greeting earlier.

"Mom, no need to fuss," Kyle said, although he clearly enjoyed the attention. "Where's Dad?"

Carol glanced around as if just becoming aware that her husband wasn't there with everyone else.

"He's in the living room with Cindy," Mark said.

As everyone headed that way Mark and Jeremiah hung back slightly.

"Why do I have a feeling that things are just going to get worse from here?" Mark asked softly.

"Because they are," Jeremiah said.

~

The evening had been miserable. Three different times Mark had tried to retreat to his and Traci's room, but she hadn't let them. He realized that they were helping to provide a buffer which terrified him. If Carol and Kyle were acting the way they were with other people around, how awful would they have been had they been alone with Cindy and Jeremiah?

The third time he'd tried to sneak off Traci had caught him at the base of the stairs and told him in no uncertain terms that it was his job to keep Jeremiah from killing Cindy's mom and brother. Mark couldn't retire for the evening until Jeremiah did.

To that end Mark had done everything he could to hint that everyone might want to get some rest. It was like some awful train wreck, though. Jeremiah thought he was staying up to protect Cindy and vice versa. He and Traci were trying to protect both of them. And he was reasonably certain given how high tensions had run that Geanie and Joseph had stayed awake just to protect their home and the various antiques that could be thrown in a fit of rage.

He'd been slow to get up in the morning. Traci had gone downstairs an hour ago and even though he was finally dressed he was still looking at excuses to delay the inevitable.

His phone rang suddenly and he snatched it off the nightstand. Maybe work needed him. It was the perfect out.

"Detective Walters speaking," he answered when he didn't recognize the incoming number.

"Detective, this is… Sadie Colbert. You came to see me a few days ago."

He was shocked to be hearing from Not Paul's former girlfriend.

"Yes, of course. What can I do for you?" he asked.

"I'm not… I'm not who you think I am," she said.

He could hear her voice shaking. He took a deep breath, struggling not to let his mind race ahead and seize on to different explanations for what she'd just said.

Just breathe and let her explain what she means, he told himself.

"Then who are you?" he asked when she didn't say anything else.

There was a sob on the other end of the line. "Not me."

"Okay."

"I have to tell you something."

"What?" he asked, his stomach starting to clench.

"Not yet. I need to see you in person, next week."

"You can't just tell me over the phone?"

"No," she whispered.

"Okay, you tell me when and where and I'll be there," he said.

"First, you have to promise me something."

"What's that?" he asked.

"You have to promise me that you'll find my son."

He had yet to hear back from his friend in child services. He didn't know if they would ultimately be able to track down Paul's son.

"I promise I'll do everything I can to find him."

"You have to. I have to know…"

"Know what?" he pressed.

There was a pause and then she said, "I'll call you in a few days."

She ended the call before he could protest.

"Who was that?" Traci asked.

"The mother of Not Paul's kid."

"It sounded like an odd conversation."

"It was," he said with a sigh. "I wish I knew what it was all about."

Traci nodded. "Speaking of odd conversations, Cindy's parents and brother went out to brunch. Joseph's ready to make the call when you are."

"Here we go," Mark said as he stood up. He followed Traci downstairs. Joseph, Geanie, Cindy, and Jeremiah were already waiting in the living room. Of all of them Joseph looked the most composed. That was probably a good thing. If he looked the way Mark was feeling at that moment there would probably be no way he could carry this off.

Mark settled himself down and Traci sat beside him. He gave Joseph a nod and the other man called Ivan then sat his phone down on the coffee table with the speaker on.

Ivan picked up halfway through the second ring. Clearly he was eager to take the call. That was hopefully a good sign.

"Joseph, you've been giving some thought to what I said?" Ivan asked, dispensing with a greeting.

"How did you know it was me? I never gave you my number," Joseph said.

It would have been disconcerting to most, but Joseph managed to sound bored and mostly disinterested even as he asked.

"I confess I got it from a mutual acquaintance at the party."

"You can never count on a socialite not to gossip about everything, particularly if they're women," Joseph said, putting just a hint of irritation into his voice.

"Yes, that's why I have yet to trust a woman's discretion."

"I'm sure you're a happier man for it," Joseph said. "So, tell me, exactly what is it you want to sell me and how will it help me with my domestic predicament?"

"Right to the point. I like that," Ivan said enthusiastically. "I'm offering you fellowship with like-minded individuals."

"Fellowship is easily purchased," Joseph said.

"Not this kind. It's a bond that goes beyond money. It's a very small group of men who have proven that they have the resolve and the wherewithal to change the world, to shape it if you will."

"If I wanted to be part of a fraternity I would have joined one in college," Joseph said.

"Ah, but the kind of fraternity I belong to would not be found at any college. Discretion is one of its chief hallmarks. Something I'm sure a man of your position can very much appreciate."

"Some days even more than others," Joseph admitted. "So, what would this society of yours have to offer me?"

"Whatever you want," Ivan said. "Business partnerships, political access, rarified amusement, and the solution to any problem you might have."

"Solutions are easy. I've found that if you throw money at problems, most of them resolve themselves quite readily."

"Unless it's a problem one happens to be married to. Traditionally there are only two ways to handle that type of problem. The first requires a rather extraordinary amount of money, enough that even you wouldn't want to part with it."

Mark could see Geanie scowling. He couldn't blame her.

"And the second?" Joseph asked.

"Connections. Connections that can help you extricate yourself quickly, quietly, with zero residual issues. Now, wouldn't that in itself hold value for you?"

Ivan was pressing in, probably hoping that he had gotten Joseph's attention and could hook him shortly.

"It would. If I could trust what you're saying."

"I'll tell you what. Why don't we meet in person to discuss this more thoroughly?" Ivan suggested.

Joseph glanced up at Mark who nodded encouragingly.

"I can make my schedule free this afternoon," Joseph said. "It's certainly a less stressful sounding way to spend an hour than watching my problem spend my money."

"I understand. I just need to make a couple of arrangements and then I can meet you anywhere you like.

"I'll meet with you at three o'clock at the lounge at The Top of the World restaurant in The World Hotel," Joseph said.

Ivan paused for a moment. "I wasn't aware they were open before dinner."

Joseph laughed. "They are for me."

Before Ivan could respond Joseph ended the call then leaned back in his chair. "Well?"

"You did a great job," Mark said. "All that time he thought he was playing you and it was you playing him."

"It sounds like he wants me to join some sort of secret society," Joseph commented.

"It sounded like that to me as well," Jeremiah said.

"I personally am not a conspiracy theorist, and I can't help but wonder if there are any secret societies left in the digital age," Mark said.

"There are," Jeremiah and Joseph said in unison.

"Okay," Mark answered. "Anything either of you want to share?"

Both men shook their heads.

"Because… secret?" Mark asked.

Both men nodded.

"I think I'm getting a headache," Mark confessed.

"So, what happens now?" Traci asked.

"Now, we get Joseph over to that lounge in plenty of time for us to station ourselves nearby."

"And then what? Get him to confess that he's murdered women before so that Joseph will believe he's capable of murdering Geanie?" Cindy asked.

"Hey!" Geanie said.

"Sorry," Cindy said with a grimace.

"First no one will say that they'd bust me out of prison and now everyone's casually discussing my future potential murder. A girl might start to feel unloved," Geanie said.

"Never unloved," Joseph said, picking up her hand and kissing the back of it.

All three women made *awww* sounds at the gesture.

"Can it, Joseph, you're making the rest of us look bad," Mark said.

"It's not my fault if other guys can't keep up," Joseph said, winking at Geanie.

~

At five minutes past three Joseph strode into the lounge at The Top of the World restaurant. Ivan was already there, seated at the only table that didn't have chairs piled on top of it. The cameras that Mark and Jeremiah had installed earlier picked up everything crystal clear.

In the limo downstairs Mark and Liam watched a video monitor intently as Ivan rose to shake Joseph's hand. Jeremiah was one floor below the restaurant, ready to spring into action if it looked like Joseph was getting into trouble.

"And the two injured players get to sit it out in the limo," Mark said with a sigh.

"I was benched once in Little League. At least these seats are a lot more comfortable," Liam said.

"You were benched? For what?"

"Punching out the umpire."

"Seriously?" Mark asked.

Just then the speaker came to life.

"Thank you for meeting me," Ivan said.

"I'll be the one thanking you if you really do have a solution to my problem," Joseph said.

"That's what we're here to discuss. Please, sit down."

Joseph sat slowly, casually, as if they were just there to discuss the weather.

"He is good at this," Liam commented.

"I hadn't noticed," Mark lied.

"Let me see if I get the gist of what you're offering," Joseph said. "Your offering me membership in your secret society."

"Wow, you get right to the point," Ivan said with a short laugh. "Essentially yes."

"And you said at the party that it wouldn't cost me money."

"That's true."

"Nothing is without a price. So, what is it you want from me in exchange?"

Ivan leaned in closer. "I want you to kill your wife."

21

A moment passed then Joseph laughed. Mark had no idea how he was staying that calm. If someone had said that to him about Traci, undercover or not he would have ended up decking the guy.

"You'll excuse me," Joseph said, "but I was under the impression that was something this society of yours could take care of for me."

"Not take care of the problem, but take care of the cleanup. And they can do it so efficiently no one will ever know what happened."

"I'm sorry, but I've been around long enough to know that when a woman ends up dead, her husband is the first suspect, no matter what."

"Ah, but the point is to not be the *last* suspect," Ivan said.

"So, what you provide me with an alibi, maybe frame someone else?" Joseph asked.

"Yes, and more."

"Forgive me if I'm skeptical. You understand, of course, that a man in my position can't afford to gamble with something like this."

"Of course you can't. That's why you need us," Ivan said, leaning closer, a look of eagerness on his face.

"And then what? The society blackmails me for the rest of my life since they know my secret?" Joseph asked.

"I can assure you that it's not like that."

"Then tell me what it is like," Joseph said, voice taking on a slight edge.

Ivan sighed and then sat back in his chair.

"We're going to lose Ivan," Mark said, starting to panic.

"I don't think so," Jeremiah said, his voice coming through the earbud in Mark's ear.

"I told you that we were bound together by a bond stronger than money," Ivan said.

"Yes, and I'm still waiting to hear what on earth you think that could be," Joseph said.

"Blood. Blood is what binds us, connects us. Blood is the cost of membership."

"I see, so killing my wife is like initiation."

"That's right," Ivan said.

"So, how did you kill your wife?" Joseph asked.

"I've never been married. It doesn't have to be a wife or a girlfriend even, but it does have to be the blood of a woman."

"Ah, so this is a gentlemen's secret society," Joseph said with just a hint of sarcasm.

Ivan shrugged. "You said it yourself. Women like to gossip, and they can't always be counted on to keep their mouths shut."

"Isn't that the truth," Joseph said wearily.

"So, interested?" Ivan asked eagerly.

Joseph sat for a moment, just staring at Ivan. Then he shook his head and stood up. "Yes, but I'll have to decline. I can't risk something like this on so little information. Good day."

"What's he doing?" Liam asked.

Joseph was almost to the door when Ivan called out, "Wait!"

Joseph turned slowly and gazed at Ivan. "I really don't think there's much more to say."

"What if I told you I'd successfully pulled this off not just for me but also for someone else? In fact, the other guy was so sloppy he got himself caught by the police through his own stupidity and in a few short days he's going to be a free man again because of me. What would you say then?"

"I'd ask if the man was that stupid why are you even bothering?" Joseph said.

"Because that's what members do for each other. Even the most brilliant among us can have an off day, make a mistake, or be trapped by our own arrogance. But, we know that others will step in to smooth things over and make sure we end up in the clear."

"It's nice to have powerful friends," Joseph said.

"It is indeed."

Joseph stood, a look of indecision on his face. Then he slowly closed his eyes. "I hate her, you know?"

"Your wife?" Ivan asked.

"Yes. So many times I've imagined what it would be like to wrap my hands around her throat and just squeeze."

Ivan moved over next to Joseph.

"It would feel good, powerful."

"Would it?" Joseph asked.

"You'd feel the life fading from her. To hold the power of life and death in your hands is like being a god."

"Did you hate the woman you killed as much as I hate my wife?" Joseph asked.

"No. I didn't even know her. She was a stripper I hired to work at my best friend's bachelor party. But I've never felt more alive than when I choked her to death. I can only imagine how much more exhilarating it will be for you given how you feel."

"We've got him," Mark breathed.

Joseph opened his eyes. "A girl you personally hired? You must have a lot of crazy going on upstairs."

"No, what I have is a whole lot of friends. We framed another guy at the party for the murder. The best part is now that he's dead we can frame him for the other woman, too. That's how my friend is getting out of his predicament."

"That is impressive," Joseph said.

"Get out of there, Joseph," Mark said.

"We've got to move," Liam urged.

"I know, I just want him clear before we take Ivan down."

"I've got a bad feeling we're not going to get that chance," Liam said.

~

Cindy felt like she was going crazy. She wasn't use to being so totally and utterly out of the loop when it came to finally catching the killer. No amount of tea that Geanie brought her or chocolate that Traci offered her could help.

"It's for the best," Traci tried once more to soothe her. "You have a broken arm. You wouldn't want to risk injuring it further.

"I just feel so helpless," Cindy said as the frustration mounted within her. She was slowly realizing that it had been a long time since she had felt this helpless. Solving mysteries, helping catch bad guys was very empowering. And now…

"It's okay. At least we distracted your family for a little while," Geanie said.

"Thanks. I could not have dealt with mom and Kyle right now."

"I'm sorry they're being so difficult," Traci said.

"I don't know why I expected otherwise."

"I don't think you expected otherwise, but I do think you were hoping that it would be better than this," Geanie said.

"You're right."

"It's okay," Geanie said. "You helped my parents come around and love Joseph. It will be the same with yours. Did you know that my mom calls him and half the time doesn't even ask to speak to me?"

Cindy laughed. "Who would have thought?"

"I know, right? And that was you. It was Cindy magic."

"I'm not feeling very magical right now," she said.

Traci gave her a half-hug. "I know it's rough being the one staying at home, waiting and wondering."

"I don't even know how you go through this day in and day out," Cindy said.

"It takes a special breed of woman to be a cop's wife," Traci said with a note of pride in her voice.

"You want to pray again?" Geanie asked.

"That's all I've been doing," Cindy said.

"Let's do it again as a group," Traci said eagerly.

Cindy glanced at her.

"What? I kind of liked it earlier," Traci said. "It felt like I was connecting to… something."

"More like Someone," Geanie noted.

"At the very least it made me feel more connected to the two of you," Traci said.

"That's not a bad thing," Cindy said.

"Exactly, so let's do the praying thing," Traci said.

"I'm sure they could use all the prayer they can get," Geanie said as she grabbed Cindy and Traci's hands.

~

Jeremiah was on the floor below the restaurant waiting for Joseph to clear the room. He could tell Mark was struggling with that as well from the bits of chatter he heard over his earbud. As for himself he was having serious déjà vu. This was the same hotel and the same floor that Cindy had been on when she'd been part of the sequestered jury trying a murder case.

"Come on, Joseph. Time to go," he said to himself.

This was taking too long. Joseph had already gotten what they needed. Why was he lingering?

"So you killed the guy you framed, too? Isn't that risky?" he heard Joseph ask.

Jeremiah closed his eyes briefly. Joseph was trying to get the guy to admit to all of it, including killing Leo.

There was a pause and Jeremiah found himself clenching his jaw while he waited for Ivan's response.

"Half of all cops are lazy and the half that aren't are overworked. They like neat. A dead guy they can blame for two murders is neat. Case closed, end of story. It makes everything so much simpler. No loose ends."

"No loose ends? Are you sure? It seems like there's always someone who knows something or has heard something," Joseph said.

There was a long pause and the hair on the back of Jeremiah's neck began to stand on end. Joseph was in

232

danger of tipping his hand. Ivan could become suspicious at any moment if he wasn't already.

When Ivan finally answered his voice was low, menacing. "I'm sure they will be taken care of."

"I'm going in," Jeremiah whispered, knowing that Mark and Liam could hear him.

Liam responded almost at once. "That's a good idea given that Mark just entered the hotel three minutes ago."

Jeremiah lunged toward the elevator. "Mark! Where are you?" he hissed.

"Two floors down," the detective said. "I've got a bad feeling this thing is about to go south."

"Ah, Mr. Joseph!" a new voice said upstairs.

Jeremiah struggled, trying to figure out who had walked in on Joseph and Ivan.

"Gustaf, hello," Joseph said, clearly startled.

"Do not mind me, I'm just here to start the dinner preparations. Do you need anything?" Gustaf asked.

"No, we're fine, thank you," Joseph said.

"That's good. Tell your lovely wife I can't wait to see her again. You know, I've never seen two people more in love than the two of them, have you?" Gustaf asked, clearly addressing Ivan.

The elevator door opened as he heard Ivan respond, "No, I haven't," in an icy cold voice.

Jeremiah punched the button that would take him upstairs directly to the restaurant. As the doors closed slowly he wished he'd taken the stairs instead. He would have been there already.

"I will see you later," Gustaf said.

A second passed and then he heard Ivan hiss, "Looks like I had the wrong idea about you."

The elevator doors slid open. He crouched down and exited the elevator at the back of the restaurant swiftly. He made his way toward the front, remaining hidden.

He could hear Ivan speaking from in front of him now as well as through the earbud.

"I think you know how this is going to end," Ivan snarled.

Jeremiah had no idea if Ivan was armed or not, but he didn't want to take any chances. The man's back came into view and Jeremiah was careful to stay out of Joseph's line of sight so as not to startle him into giving away Jeremiah's presence.

"But you don't!" Mark called, stepping suddenly into view.

Ivan spun with an oath and threw Joseph into Mark. He then raced past them toward the main elevators as the two men fell. Jeremiah leaped forward, but was a split second too late to catch Ivan before the doors closed on the elevator he ran into.

Jeremiah turned and dashed for the stairs. It was a long way down, but it was his only shot at catching Ivan before he disappeared downstairs. "Liam! He's heading down in the elevator!" Jeremiah exclaimed as he vaulted over the railing partway down the first flight and landed on the second.

"On it," he heard Liam answer tersely.

Jeremiah continued downward, bypassing as many of the stairs as he could without risking injury. He could hear Mark and Joseph in his earbud but didn't take time to respond. He focused all his efforts on making it to the lobby before Ivan.

When he finally crashed through the door into the lobby he spun around, scanning to see if he saw Ivan before heading toward the elevator bank. An elevator opened and a woman ran out, screaming. She was followed by another woman and Ivan who had his tie wrapped around her throat and was choking her. He stared right at Jeremiah as he stepped off the elevator.

"Back!" he hissed.

The woman was starting to turn blue in the face. He had already cut off her oxygen. There were just moments left before she'd black out and collapse. When that happened she'd fall and Ivan wouldn't be able to hide behind her. If he rushed in she could get hurt. All he had to do was wait those few seconds.

Ivan started half-dragging her toward the front doors. It was midday and there were only a few people in the lobby, most of them employees who were just starting to realize that there was a problem. Ivan kept his eyes pinned to Jeremiah.

Which was why he didn't see Liam walk up behind him. Liam hit him in the head with the butt of his gun and Ivan fell, losing his grip on the woman who slid to the floor. Jeremiah ran forward and yanked the tie from around her neck. She gasped and started coughing.

Ivan was dazed but still conscious. He looked up at Liam.

"Who are you?" Ivan demanded.

"I'm one of those overworked cops you talked about, only I don't like neat. I like truth, no matter how messy it is," Liam said as he awkwardly handcuffed him using just the hand on his good arm. He then started reading him his rights as Jeremiah got the woman up and over onto one of the chairs.

Mark and Joseph came running out of another elevator a few seconds later. "Thank heavens," Joseph said when he saw that Liam had Ivan subdued.

"Even an injured cop was more than enough to take care of this trash," Mark said with satisfaction.

"What am I being charged with?" Ivan demanded.

"Well, for starters, the murder of April Snow. And I'm pretty sure we can tack a few more on there, like Beau, Leo, heck, maybe even Rose's roommate. Oh and there's conspiracy to commit murder in the case of Cindy Preston. I'm sure the list will just keep going from there."

Ivan began to laugh. "You think you're so clever, don't you, Detective? But at the end of the day, you don't know anything."

"I know more than enough to get you convicted," Mark said as he bent down and grabbed Ivan, yanking him up onto his feet.

"Liam, why don't you put this trash in the car while I take some statements?" Mark asked.

"Glad to," Liam said, hauling Ivan toward the front door.

Mark turned toward him and noticed the woman that Jeremiah was tending to. "Is she okay?"

"Ivan attacked her, was using her," Jeremiah said.

"Son of a-"

A sudden shout from the front door caused Jeremiah to twist around just in time to see Liam collapse onto his knees just outside the hotel entrance while Ivan took off running.

Jeremiah sprang into action followed by Mark.

"He's trying to get away!" Mark shouted.

A moment later Jeremiah realized that Ivan's purpose was much darker. "Stop, Ivan!" he shouted as the man perched for a second on the curb. The man glanced over his shoulder at Jeremiah, smirked, and then threw himself into the road, directly in front of a bus.

~

It was three hours before Jeremiah, Joseph, Mark, and Liam were free to leave the scene. Ivan had died seconds after being hit by the bus. Once they were done Liam headed home and the rest of them headed back to Joseph's.

"So, he's behind not only the stripper's death, but also the deaths of everyone that could help convict his pal, Cartwright," Mark said wearily.

"Nice and neat," Joseph said, sounding more than a little shell-shocked.

"Too neat," Jeremiah muttered.

"I have to admit that he was right about one thing," Mark said.

"What's that?" Joseph asked.

"I like neat. Closed cases, that sort of thing."

"So, we're letting this go?" Jeremiah asked.

"I don't see that we have much of a choice," Mark said.

"Unless someone still tries to kill you or Cindy," Jeremiah said with clenched jaw. "What then?"

"Then it was definitely Cartwright's fiancée behind all that," Mark said.

"Waiting to see if the two of you get attacked doesn't seem like a great plan," Joseph said.

"No, but it's the only one I got at the moment," Mark admitted. "Maybe things will be different in the morning."

They finally arrived at the house. Jeremiah was bone weary and more than a little worried. He wanted a shower and a meal but more than anything he wanted to see Cindy.

Jeremiah walked into the living room, hoping to find her there. Back in the kitchen Geanie and Traci were kissing their husbands and at the moment a kiss from Cindy sounded like the best thing in the world to him.

When he walked in, a figure got up from the couch and with a surge of disappointment he realized it was Kyle.

"Hey, do you know where Cindy is?" he asked.

"I would never tell you even if I knew," Kyle hissed, his face contorted in anger.

22

"Do you have something to say, Kyle?" Jeremiah asked, working hard to keep his voice neutral.

Kyle stared at him for a long moment, a muscle in his jaw working. "I wish I was one of those tough, scary guys."

"Why?"

"Because then I could make you leave my sister alone."

Jeremiah took a deep breath. "Kyle, don't worry about it. There isn't a person on this planet that could make me leave Cindy alone."

He had meant it to be reassuring, but it clearly had the opposite affect. Kyle blanched and took a step back.

Jeremiah sighed. "Look, I know you don't like me. Frankly, the feeling is pretty much mutual. But I think we need to try to get along for Cindy's sake."

Kyle shook his head and took another step backward. "You're poison. Yet here you are, asking me to smile and pretend that it isn't true? I won't do that, even if you kill me for it."

"I'm not going to kill you," Jeremiah said, taking a step forward.

Kyle backpedaled more, trying to stay out of arm's reach. It was a vain attempt. He had no idea just how fast Jeremiah could move. If he wanted to hurt Kyle he could do it before the other man even realized it was coming.

"Can we at least agree that we both love Cindy?" Jeremiah asked, struggling with impatience. There were real threats out there to be countered while he was engaged in this pointless dance with Kyle. Still, for Cindy's sake, he had to try.

"I love her. I'm not sure what I'd call your feelings for her," Kyle said defiantly.

"Look, I know you've been hurt. I know you care about Cindy. I'm taking both of those into consideration. You love her and I love her. The truth is, she chose me and nothing either you or I can say will change her mind. At the end of the day we both need to respect her decision even if we disagree with it."

"You can drop the 'we' part. I know you're just talking about me."

It showed just how much Kyle didn't know or understand him. Jeremiah still had times when he felt Cindy was wrong to want to be with him. He was lecturing himself just as much as he was lecturing the other man.

"Can *we* at least try to be civil to each other when she's around?" Jeremiah asked.

Kyle narrowed his eyes. "I can try," he said at last.

"That's all I'm asking for."

Kyle nodded. "If you hurt my sister in any way I'll find one of those scary guys to kill you."

"If I hurt your sister, you won't have to," Jeremiah said softly.

Kyle turned abruptly and left the room. Jeremiah sat down on the couch. There was nothing he could do to change Kyle's mind about him. Nor would he keep trying to. It was a waste of energy. He just hoped that Kyle would follow through on his intention to be civil in Cindy's presence. The last thing Jeremiah wanted was for her to suffer because the two of them couldn't stand each other.

He glanced up as he heard a soft footstep. Cindy's father, Don, walked into the room. He didn't look surprised to see Jeremiah there.

"I wondered why Kyle had such a sour look on his face," he said.

Jeremiah winced inwardly. It was bad enough that they'd had to cut all potential future ties with his family. He didn't want to burn bridges with Cindy's, too. That wasn't fair to her.

"He attempted to have a talk with me man-to-man."

To his surprise Don chuckled softly. "That must have been painful to watch."

"Something like that."

"Mind if I sit?"

"Please do," Jeremiah said.

Don settled himself down into a nearby chair and sat sizing up Jeremiah for a moment. "Back in Las Vegas I told my daughter that you were a dangerous man."

"And?" Jeremiah asked, dreading where the conversation seemed to be going.

"She said she knew. And it was pretty clear to me that she had already made her mind up even then. She loves you, you know."

"I love her, too."

"I know. I can tell. I could tell back then. For a man who has done the types of things you surely have done you have a terrible poker face."

"Only when it comes to Cindy."

"She's your kryptonite. I get it. I really do."

"And?" Jeremiah asked hesitantly.

"And I've never seen her happier than when she's with you. After her sister died she withdrew from the world. There wasn't anything that I could do for her it seemed. I tried, but she just kept retreating, becoming obsessed with being safe. It broke my heart. I didn't want her to be afraid of life. I wanted her to embrace it. I didn't know how to help her. Then you came along and everything changed."

"It changed for me, too," Jeremiah said as the older man paused.

"I can imagine. Men like you tend to be fairly solitary. Sharing your life with someone can't be easy. It's probably a choice you're making day by day."

"Very few worthwhile things are easy," Jeremiah said softly.

"No, they're not. Look, I'm going to be straight with you. You're never going to win over Kyle or Cindy's mom."

"I had that distinct impression."

"To be honest, I wouldn't even try at this point. It's just a waste of everyone's time. I know that sounds harsh, but I know my wife. I know my son. They're both rigid, inflexible in the way they think. Frankly, it will take an act of God to make them come around."

"At least I know where I stand with them," Jeremiah said.

Don smiled faintly. "And you deserve to know where you stand with me. I won't lie to you, I worry about my daughter and her safety, particularly now that she seems to be solving a mystery every other holiday. I worry a lot less knowing that you're here to protect her."

"I don't know what to say, sir."

"Say that you'll keep her up on that pedestal you've got her on for the rest of your life."

"I will."

"Say that you'll always love, cherish, and protect her."

"With everything that I am," Jeremiah vowed.

Don's smile broadened. "And don't call me sir. Call me Dad, or Don if you can't stomach that."

Jeremiah sucked in his breath. "I'd like that very much, Dad."

"Good. Now, do me a favor. Don't ever mention to Cindy's mom that you used to work for the Mossad."

"I don't know what you're talking about," Jeremiah said evenly.

Don laughed. "Okay, so you do have a poker face when we're not talking about Cindy. Glad to see it. Otherwise you'd never beat her at cards and I'm counting on you to help me trounce her and Carol at pinochle."

"I've never played before."

"Don't worry, something tells me you're a fast learner. Competitive, too, unless I miss my guess."

"It has been said."

Don made as if to rise, but then hesitated and sat back down. "If you don't mind my asking, Cindy hasn't said anything about your family."

Jeremiah nodded. "They aren't in the picture."

"May I ask why?"

Jeremiah studied the other man, debating what to tell him. Finally he sighed. "At first it was for their safety."

"Uh huh. I figured as much. Something changed, though, didn't it?"

Jeremiah nodded. "Through a series of very unexpected events Cindy met them last summer."

"It didn't go well?"

"No, but that was more about me than her."

"The fact that she was a Christian couldn't have helped, though."

"That is correct."

"How did it end?"

"Let's just say that I have only one man I can call father at this point. It's you."

Don winced. "I'm sorry to hear that. Puts some pressure on me. I hope I can live up to it."

"I have a feeling you're more than equal to the challenge."

"I'll make you a deal. As long as you're straight with me, I'll be straight with you."

"I can't promise-"

"I'm not asking you to tell me anything about your job, past or future. I'm asking you to be honest with me about where you're at, mentally, emotionally."

Jeremiah glanced down for a moment. He knew that the other man was offering him a gift. His hesitation in accepting it had everything to do with the life he'd lived and the struggle he was still enduring to let others in even now.

"You're a smart, observant man," he said at last.

"I'll take the compliment," Don said.

"You're right to assume that I have a hard time being… forthcoming with that kind of information."

"There's an understatement."

"I deeply appreciate your offer. It's more than I could expect. Frankly, more than I deserve."

"But?" Don asked.

"Trusting others in this sort of way is a new thing for me. I don't want to let you down."

Don looked away for a moment. When he looked back there were tears glistening in his eyes. "You love her with everything you have in you and treat her like she deserves. As long as you do that, there's nothing you can do to let me down."

Jeremiah's throat constricted. "Thank you."

It was all he could think to say.

Don reached out and grabbed his arm. "Thank *you*."

He let go just as Cindy walked into the room. She paused, a worried look passing over her face. "Is everything okay?" she asked, the apprehension clear in her voice.

"Dad and I were just talking," Jeremiah said, smiling.

"Dad?" she asked, clearly startled.

"Of course, 'Dad'. What else is he going to call me?" Don asked. "We were just discussing how we're going to slaughter you and your mother at pinochle."

"What? Jeremiah's going to be my partner."

Don laughed. "You're wrong there. We have a time-honored tradition in this family, passed down by your grandparents. When it comes to cards, it's boys versus girls. And now that you were kind enough to find me a good partner, the girls' days of winning are over."

"Jeremiah!" Cindy exclaimed, clearly hoping that he would take her side.

He smirked and met her father's eyes. The older man was enjoying this.

"Sorry, hon, but your traditions are now my traditions. Besides, your dad's been saddled with a lousy partner in your brother long enough."

"That much is certain," Don said fervently. "That boy can do a lot of things but he can't play cards worth a darn. It's embarrassing."

Cindy smirked. "Okay, time to go."

"Go where?" Don asked.

"Joseph's taking us all out to eat to celebrate."

"Lead the way," he said.

~

"Your stomach's growling," Traci whispered.

"I can't help it, I'm hungry," Mark replied.

They were standing with Joseph and Geanie in the foyer, waiting for everyone else to show up so they could head out to dinner. Finally Cindy, Jeremiah, and Don arrived from the direction of the living room.

"Just waiting on two," Mark said. Frankly, the two they were waiting on were the two he'd like to leave behind. He managed to bite his tongue and not say so, but the urge was nearly overwhelming.

Joseph's phone rang and the other man pulled it out of his pocket.

"Hello," Joseph said answering his phone. He quickly frowned and pulled the phone away from his ear. He hit the speaker button. "Who is this?" he asked.

A low, raspy voice that was clearly disguised answered. "A former friend and colleague of Ivan's."

There was a look of panic on Joseph's face, but his voice was steady. "It's a shame what happened to him."

"Yes, it is."

"What do you want?"

"A few days ago Ivan recommended you as someone who might make a great addition to our little… club."

"And?" Joseph prompted.

"And, we agree."

"Meaning what, exactly?" Joseph asked.

"Meaning that we will be in touch soon."

The caller hung up and they all stood for a moment in stunned silence. Finally, Joseph broke it. "What have I done?"

"I don't know, but I have a bad feeling about this," Mark said.

"A bad feeling about what?" Kyle asked as he came down the stairs accompanied by Carol.

Mark glanced at Cindy's family and was at a loss for what to say. Before anyone could come up with anything to say there was a sudden pounding on the front door.

"Who on earth could that be?" Joseph muttered. He moved to the door and opened it.

From where he was standing Mark could see Detective Keenan. The other detective pushed past Joseph and half a dozen uniformed officers came in after him.

"What is going on here?" Joseph demanded, anger filling his voice.

Mark stared, thunderstruck, wondering what on earth was going on.

Detective Keenan strode forward purposefully. "Jeremiah Silverman, you're under arrest."

Everyone gasped as two officers grabbed Jeremiah and tried to cuff him. Panic surged through Mark as he saw the rabbi's muscles tense. The other man was about to react and it was going to turn out badly if he did.

"What is going on here?" Mark demanded of Keenan.

"Exactly what it looks like. We're arresting this man."

"Why?" Cindy burst out.

"You have the right to remain silent," Kennan began, addressing Jeremiah.

"There has to be some mistake. Let's discuss this," Mark pleaded.

"Anything you say can and will be used against you in a court of law. You have the right to an attorney. If you can't-"

"Stop this!" Mark roared.

Keenan blinked and then kept right on going. Cindy tried to move to Jeremiah's side but officers blocked her way. Jeremiah looked like a man trapped. His fists clenched and Mark prayed that Jeremiah wasn't armed.

"It will be okay," Cindy said, her voice ringing out above Keenan's droning recitation of Jeremiah's rights. "We'll figure this out."

"Yes, we will," Mark hastened to lend his voice, hoping to calm his friend down before he struck or killed one of the officers. "Jeremiah, it's going to be okay, I promise."

Something dark glimmered in the depths of the other man's eyes and Mark sucked in his breath.

"Jeremiah, please!" Cindy pleaded.

Jeremiah blinked, turned and looked at her, and took a shuddering breath. He went still and the officers were able to cuff him. He turned and stared at Keenan as the man finished giving him his rights.

"What am I being arrested for?" Jeremiah asked, his voice low and tight.

Keenan stared at him for an endless moment before finally spitting out a single word. "Murder."

Debbie Viguié is the New York Times Bestselling author of more than four dozen novels including the *Wicked* series, the *Crusade* series and the *Wolf Springs Chronicles* series co-authored with Nancy Holder. Debbie also writes thrillers including *The Psalm 23 Mysteries,* the *Kiss* trilogy, and the *Witch Hunt* trilogy. When Debbie isn't busy writing she enjoys spending time with her husband, Scott, visiting theme parks. They live in Florida with their cat, Schrödinger.

Made in the USA
San Bernardino, CA
22 June 2018